Also by Kathleen Stauffer

*We See In a Mirror Dimly*

*The Secret Is*

*All the Rivers Run Into the Sea*

*Thou Shalt Not*

*Do Not Be Deceived*

# SUMMONED

*Kathleen Stauffer*

**WESTBOW**
PRESS®
A DIVISION OF THOMAS NELSON
& ZONDERVAN

This is a work of fiction. All of the characters, names, incidents, organizations, and dialogue in this novel are either the products of the author's imagination or are used fictitiously.

WestBow Press books may be ordered through booksellers or by contacting:

WestBow Press
A Division of Thomas Nelson & Zondervan
1663 Liberty Drive
Bloomington, IN 47403
www.westbowpress.com
1 (866) 928-1240

ISBN: 978-1-9736-5840-5 (sc)
ISBN: 978-1-9736-5842-9 (hc)
ISBN: 978-1-9736-5841-2 (e)

Library of Congress Control Number: 2019903841

Print information available on the last page.

WestBow Press rev. date: 4/4/2019

# ACKNOWLEDGEMENTS

I'd like to thank the following people for their support, encouragement, and prayers. A respectful tribute to Connie Lee, plot analyst, who has a knack for pulling all things together during the final steps. My appreciation to first readers Bab Augusta, Mary Ann Abel, and Donna Gritten-Harmon, long-time friends and avid readers, for their perceptions. A special heart-felt appreciation to husband, David, who puts up with a wife whose fingertips are often tapping away at a keyboard. And lastly, my gratitude to editor, Jed Magee, master of flash fiction and Haiku, who helped shape the entire final draft.

# AUTHOR COMMENTS

Although many of these stories are inspired by true life events, each is a work of creative writing with names, characters, places, incidents, dialogue, internal motivations, and thoughts being a part of the author's imagination and written in a fictitious manner. Similarities or likenesses to real people or places are coincidental.

Kathleen Stauffer

# CONTENTS

Summoned .................................................................... 1

Jacqueline's Story: Do Not Fear ............................... 55

Ramona's Visitor ....................................................74

Hope ............................................................................ 81

Norma's Class Reunion ....................................... 100

Once Upon a Time ................................................ 111

Providence .............................................................. 144

Divine Plan ............................................................. 150

Discussion Questions .......................................... 151

*But now, this is what the LORD says—*

*He who created you, O Jacob,*

*He who formed you, O Israel:*

*"Fear not, for I have redeemed you;*

*I have summoned you by name;*

*you are mine."*

*Isaiah 43:1*

# PROLOGUE

The phrase *hit and run* fled in muted tones up and down the halls, lingered by the lockers and restrooms, and scuttled at the end of the day onto the busses on a cold winter day. As a senior in high school, I couldn't stop thinking, *what a horrible way to die*—out on a country road, staring up at the stars, unable to move, and wondering how God could allow this to happen. Strangers found eighteen-year-old Michael lying along the side of County Road B 20. *Whoever ran over him must have known him*, or so everyone said. *Otherwise, his arms wouldn't have been crossed over his chest lying so neatly by the roadside.*

I run my fingertips over the rough edges of his grave stone and consider how his death and the secrets behind it continue to plague his family and friends.

Curiosity over Michael's circumstances provided an atmosphere of confusion for months although we stopped talking about it. One spring day in the school library, I pulled the book, "What's In a Name?" from a dusty shelf and found *Michael*. Derived from the Hebrew designation, it belonged to one of the seven archangels—the one closest to God and responsible for carrying out God's judgements. The name means, *Who is like God?* –a rhetorical question implying *no one is like God*. This new knowledge only scattered my perceptions, or should I say, misperceptions.

At the time of Michael's misfortune, I did not know that my own life would also end tragically and unresolved.

# 1

I come often to a country cemetery on the edge of a little town I once was a part of. My footsteps are light; there is no worn footpath. I approach Michael's headstone and kneel reverently. There are other names I recognize, Grandmother Hulda and Grandfather Arthur, who lived worthy hard-working lives into their eighties. Pay-attention-to-me twitters rise from a nearby ancient oak. I glance up to a wisp of brilliant red thrashing about as if caught in the branches but continue my short journey to the spot I am most familiar. Dropping before the cold, granite stone, I study the flowers surrounding a cross imprinted in the left hand corner and focus on the engraved letters: Emilie Fischer, November 17, 1957 – October 23, 1976. Another eighteen-year-old girl whose life was cut short. **God Bless Our Daughter** is engraved at the very bottom. If I could feel agony, it would be here, with this phrase. You see, I *was* Emilie.

I attended my funeral and followed the casket down the aisle while the congregation sang, "Blessed assurance, Jesus is mine…." At least, *some* sang; others gazed in disbelief at the box covered with flowers that held the lifeless body of an eighteen year old girl. The church was full. I had not seen it so full, not even on Christmas Eve or Easter Sunday. Dressed in black and holding white hankies, my friends, some of my teachers, the sheriff, and people I did not even know showed up. I placed my transformed self on the red carpeted steps leading up to the altar, chin in my cupped hands, while Pastor Snider read from scripture, *For My thoughts are not your thoughts, neither are your ways My ways, saith the LORD.*

At the burial site, my mother's despairing wails, snagged by the wind and resonating from one grave marker to another, intermixed with the reverend's words, "I am the resurrection and the life. He who believes in me will live, even though he dies, and whoever lives and believes in me will never die." My father held her shaking shoulders as someone scooped up a shovel of dirt that made the first thump on my casket. I wanted to console her; I wanted to tell her, *it's okay*. But, I couldn't; it wasn't.

Mourners walked unsteadily to their cars and returned to the church basement for ham sandwiches, cake, coffee, and indistinct conversations. On their way home, their minds tried to comprehend the fine line that separates the living from the dead. Parents spent more time tucking their children into bed that evening and remembered to pray with them, *Now I lay me down to sleep, I pray the Lord my soul to keep....* Holding each other tight, they slept in brief, troubled snatches, worried about the future of their own precious children, the decisions they would make and how little control they really had over life.

In spite of a short life, what I did have was mostly pleasant. I grew up among fields of corn and beans waving in morning sunlight. I had a pony, not much good for riding, but a worthy companion. My parents took me to Minnesota and an emerald lake surrounded with majestic evergreens where we fished and swam and returned home with sun-kissed skin and smelling of lake water. I watched jet streaks cross the sky and dreamed of far-off-places, but never took a flight anywhere. I don't need to now; I can go almost anywhere I want to just by thinking about it. But mostly I decide to stay where I am, in this small area where a tragedy happened long enough ago.

My mother used to tell me, among other things, that curiosity killed the cat. Curiosity, along with a hint of rebellion, probably got me into the situation on that country road. *Who, what, where, when, why,* were questions everyone asked. *Why me? ....* Before I really go, I want to figure this out.

••••••••

# 2

*"For My thoughts are not your thoughts, neither are your ways My ways," saith the LORD.* I chose Isaiah 55:8 for my eighth grade confirmation verse because I was rebellious and determined that this verse might be a message to my parents. I was not like them. I did not think like them and disliked the fact that they expected me to reason the way they did. However, my attitude was slightly transformed during the sermon that Sunday in May.

"Just go ahead with what you've been given," Pastor Snider stated authoritatively. *With what you've been given?* I had not been given what others in my class had—the color of hair, the way they talked, their mannerisms came from their parents. "You received Jesus Christ, the Master; now *live* in Him. You're deeply rooted in Him. By this time, you know your way in the faith. Now go out and do what you've been taught. Confirmation is done," Pastor Snider said and smiled at us and understood we were all relieved. "You can quit studying and start living it. Boots on the ground!" He exhaled noisily, after using one of his favored phrases having been a military chaplain in his younger years.

The once nicely pressed white gown hung limply on my fourteen-year-old body. My pink carnation corsage had wilted. I was anxious to get home to a roasting chicken in the oven, mashed potatoes, and Mom's home-made apple pie; put on some comfortable clothes and pull my hair back in a ponytail.

"Dad and I are proud of you, Emilie," Mom said on our way home. She turned around in the front seat to wink at me and to make sure I had heard her. Her hair was brushed back and kept in place with combs; her hair was graying. She had never colored her hair and didn't believe in makeup or nail polish. I returned her smile; she was an okay mom.

"You take your profession of faith seriously, and it will all fall into place for you," my dad added with a wink of his own in the rearview mirror. "There'll be a few bumps in the road, but God will get you where you need to go." Farmer talk, I thought, *bumps in the road?* I was surrounded by men who were dull, predictable, passive, and conservative. Although I appreciated my dad's gentle spirit, I also found him to be boring, tied to routine, prudent. There was not a spontaneous cell in his body.

*My* parents, I thought; but, not really. The same old questions worried my brain. *Didn't my mother want me? Where is she now?* The word *illegitimate* stung. As a young child, I overheard a teacher at school use it in reference to me. At home, I asked my mom what it meant. "Where did you hear that?" she asked and acted like I had slapped her on the face. "Out of wedlock," she mumbled as I continued to stare at her. *Out of wedlock* was just as foreign as the word illegitimate at the time, and I let it go. I was the only adopted kid in school; it's a little like Hester Prynne having to wear an A to mark her shame. I wasn't ashamed; I was curious about my biological family, confused that it was treated like a secret, and, yes, sometimes angry. I had a caring adoptive family; I just knew I was different.

There were other thoughts, more fun. After all, I was only fourteen and not too worried about a few bumps in the road and God getting me to where I needed to go. I had a special interest in someone in my confirmation class: David. I had looked up the definition of his name, and it means *beloved*. And, I did beloved him. We smiled at each other, exchanged notes in school, and pressed our fingertips together when passing in the halls sending tingles like tiny firecrackers.

When we were both sixteen and David had use of his parents' car, we started dating. *The Sound of Music, Doctor Zhivago, Major Dundee*—each eventually made it to the Starlight, the drive-in movie theater in our area. Buttered popcorn, syrupy sodas, sticky hands, and goodnight kisses. I thought about him almost constantly to the point that my grades were slipping.

"What's this?" my father asked after report card day. We were eating supper, the three of us. Hamburger and potato casserole with homemade bread and canned green beans from the garden beside our house.

"Hmmm?" I murmured and realized the chocolate cake with creamy fudge frosting for dessert would not be enjoyed as it was typically.

"You've always had As and Bs. You're slipping, Emilie Fischer. Too much time with David?"

"No, of course not." I stalled, my attitude taking a nose-dive with my dad's use of my first *and* last name. He did this when he wanted to make an impression on me.

*Fischer's not my real last name,* I said inside my head while thinking of an excuse. "We had this really hard test and I forgot to study."

"Forgetfulness? I think not." Dad rubbed his whiskered chin, took out his farmer hankie, blew his nose, and then wiped his brow. Would I be grounded? Butterflies were taking wing in my stomach. I knew I had to come up with a solution or I would not be seeing David for a while.

"I'll take care of it, Dad," I promised and stacked the dishes and silverware while Mom filled the sink with hot water and soap. I noticed her hands and how different they were than mine: smallish with blunted fingers, already discolored with spidery veins crisscrossing each other. My hands were narrow with longer fingers. My parents didn't get me; they didn't understand; I did not come from them. Somehow, it made it easier for me to be contentious.

I plunged my hands into the hot, soapy water and grabbed a fistful of silverware, whished it around a bit, and then dropped it into the rinse water. I knew this frustrated my mother; she washed each piece of silverware individually, checked the tines of each fork meticulously.

"Make sure," Dad answered. The back screen door slapped shut. Mom took out a dish towel and sang softly, "Blessed assurance, Jesus is mine, oh what a foretaste of glory divine…" as if she were looking forward to heaven, her earthly existence with a teenaged daughter being so trying. The chocolate cake remained on the countertop next to the leftovers, untouched, except by an errant fly.

I no longer skipped doing homework and studied diligently for tests. David and I kept seeing each other every Saturday night—going to the movies, looping Main Street, and hanging out with friends. We explored the gravel roads and even ventured over to Big Stone Lake to look for good places to talk.

"What do you want to be when you grow up?" I asked one night. We were both turned in our seats, facing each other, fingers entwined.

"A pilot." He smiled and pointed to the sky. "See that light."

"Which one?" I asked and peered through the front window of the car. "The sky is full of them."

"The light that is moving," he explained. "See it."

"I do. It's a plane, right?"

"A jet," David corrected. "That'll be me some day."

I watched the jet, light blinking, high above us among the stars, and imagined flying to England, to France, or some remote island with David. We would see the world together.

A person can only ask *what do you want to be when you grow up* once or twice, and, then, especially when conversations are held under the stars and in the backseat of a car, other things happen. Talking lead to necking, necking led to desire. *I love you* was whispered back and forth and in between wet kisses, but what do two teenagers know of love especially with hormones raging. But, he needed more than I could give or maybe I needed more than he could give. We would end up arguing about really dumb stuff, like what time he was going to pick me up, or what we were going to do. Several times, he took me home early, and I understood rejection on a new level. He left for the state university and I attended junior college. Letters were exchanged but not often. The phone calls stopped. A friendly card arrived for Valentine's Day which I promptly dumped in the waste paper basket.

When grocery shopping with my mother, I spotted TEEN magazine. The headlines, *A Heavenly Guide to Boys* and *Weekly Beauty Workouts* got my attention. I dropped it in the grocery cart under my mother's raised eyebrows. At home, I devoured every page and advertisement and spent the next month experimenting with hair, makeup, and a new me. At about the same time, I saw the ad in the local newspaper for the Miss County Queen contest and entered myself. Maybe my relationship with David could be rekindled. I decided to give him the good news and called him myself.

"Hi, how's school going?" I asked.

"Same old, same old," he answered. "And, you?"

"It's okay, not much new." He didn't seem real excited that I had called. The pauses were too long. "I did something kind of crazy," I said, my palms suddenly sweaty.

"You? Yeah, right. You don't have a crazy bone in you," he replied.

"I've entered the county queen competition."

David said nothing.

"Are you still there?"

"Why would you do that?" He asked, sounding miffed.

"Why *wouldn't* I do it?"

"It just doesn't sound like you," he said. My heart withered.

"Well, I am…" I felt meek, mousy, and no longer sure of my decision.

"Hey, okay." He rushed his words. "We probably need to talk. You gonna be home this weekend?"

"Maybe; what do you want to do?" My stomach was sinking and I knew why. David had stopped loving me. He didn't care. Anymore.

"I'll be out Saturday, around 7," David said and hung up.

And that's when this precious boyfriend of mine broke up with me. Using the excuse that we were going to different colleges and keeping up a long-distance relationship was difficult, he stumbled through his monologue. Even though things had gone a little flat, I thought I had a future with David—a guy who wanted to become a pilot. A guy who had showed me his dad's plane and said that one day he'd take me up. A guy who once upon a time was crazy about me. We'd sing our song, *Sugarpie, honey bunch… can't help myself… love you and nobody else* off-key and then laugh until our sides ached. We'd hang out at the Roof Top on Big Stone Lake, watch the waves lap the shore. But, David, my beloved, broke up with me.

"We should see other people," he had said. Rumors travel in a small town, and the name, Patricia, had been used when David's name came up. David's excuse was lousy; he was *already* seeing someone else. Patricia had been on the homecoming court the year after we graduated. Her family had a huge Victorian house with a wraparound porch on the edge of town. White fences enclosed a few horses. She drove a Ford Mustang that all the boys envied. And, she had had eyes on David for a long time.

I lived in a simple farm house. My folks had a station wagon which I wasn't allowed to drive. But, I was prettier than Patricia, and I knew it. I wanted him to want me back; I had something to prove.

———— ◆◆◆◆◆ ————

# 3

Patricia Schomberg, David's new girl, became Miss County Queen. With a name like Patricia, it seems a girl has an advantage when it comes to queen competitions; Patricia means *noble*. Emilie, my name, means *industrious, thriving*; and I decided to succeed and bloom in my own way. My picture made the newspaper, I was in the parade, and all the candidates stood in a line in the school gymnasium before the crowning. I noticed David sitting with Patricia's parents. I raised my chin a few notches and let my eyes rove the back of the gym where a few hung out in the bleachers. An older, good looking guy sat by himself, elbows on his knees, scrutinizing the stage where eight girls stood, dressed in gowns, their hair and makeup perfect. He appeared restless, agitated in an Elvis Presley cool kind of way. Elvis' song, *It's Now or Never*, zinged through me. Our eyes connected briefly, and I felt excitement, curiosity, and a sense of adventure.

Weeks later, when looping Main Street with friends, I saw this same guy standing in front of Mikey's, a bar in town. The car windows were down, and I stared at him until he noticed me, my head half way out the window. We made eye contact. He yelled, "Hey Emilie!" I dropped back into my seat, dumbfounded.

"You know *Terry Wilson*?" someone asked.

"Bad boy. Gotta a reputation, girl chaser," Barb, the girl beside me, said and blushed. Everyone was shocked that Terry knew my name.

"How does he know *you*?" Cindy asked.

"I, I'm not sure," I lied but knew I had initiated the whole thing.

"He's too old for you, Emilie," another said.

"I heard he was married," my friend, Mary, commented. My lips were still, but my heart was sprinting.

He called me a week later. Mom answered the phone. She usually did.

"Yes, this is the Fischers," she replied crisply. "Emilie? You want *Emilie*? Who is this please?"

"Mom!" I said and grabbed the phone from her. She stayed by my side.

"This is Emilie," I murmured, embarrassed.

"Hi, this is Terry. Terry Wilson." His husky voice scrambled my emotions.

"Are you still there?" he asked. My mother breathed down my neck.

"Yes, I'm here." I could barely whisper. I never imagined the guy would call me.

"I'm not sure if you know me or not…." His voice was soft, engaging.

"I know you," I answered quietly. Very quietly. I thought about hanging up.

"Just wondering if you wanted to go out sometime," he said.

"Maybe," I answered. My mother was a foot away, her arms crossed, wearing her mad face.

"This weekend work?" he asked.

"No," I replied. I was scared stiff and handed my mother the phone.

"What have you just done?" Mother asked and dropped the phone as if it were a snake. I heard the receiver clunk to the floor and then the dial tone.

"I *said* 'no'," I replied, marched out of the kitchen, took the steps two at a time to my room, and threw myself on the bed. I felt frustrated, small-town bored, and isolated from everything the world could offer. Our small community had had its notables. A couple of major league baseball players, a Dallas sports radio announcer. But basically it was a community where people were neighborly, went to work each day, and came home to rest and take care of their families. Surrounded by farms and a few country churches, it was a safe and secure environment. I was tired of safe and secure.

The bed squeaked as Mom settled beside me and started rubbing my back. "What happened to David?" she asked.

"Mom, David is history. Haven't you noticed? He hasn't been around for months."

"Well, yes, I guess. It's just that you never mentioned what happened. I thought maybe it didn't matter." She was trying, I could tell. I wanted to be mean to her and yet she was undeserving of my bitter attitude.

"You know," she said. "It's best to ignore much of what a young man says to you. But, better yet, pay attention to how he treats not only you but other people." Was she referring to Terry Wilson? Was his reputation really that bad?

Like I said, she was trying. I didn't want to bring up the fact that David was treating Patricia Schomberg very well and probably saying all the right things, too. The bed tilted to its normal position as she got up and took the steps down to the kitchen where she typically spent most of her day. Cooking, baking, dusting, hanging our laundry out on the line for the world to see was her life. She was a stay-at-home mom; I couldn't imagine a more dreary life. Sounds from the kitchen snuck up the steps. The clutter of pots and pans being pulled from the cabinets for another meal, the refrigerator door opening and closing, Dad coming up the back steps with a weather report. As I stared at the fading daisies on the wallpaper, my thoughts drifted, and I couldn't help but wonder what my *real* momma might be doing, where we would be living, and how I could be spending my days. The tears came one by one. I counted them as each dropped from my chin while supper smells filled the house. Outside, the windmill twisted in the wind, a melancholy song. I heard my dad pull the barn door shut and latch it. Going to the window, I noted a few thunderheads hunched on the horizon.

"Emilie, supper's ready," Mom called from the bottom of the steps.

"Give me a minute," I answered and watched the sky grow dark.

I returned to my dorm life and the community college classes with clean laundry and leftovers that Mom had carefully labeled and packed for me. Terry Wilson somehow found my phone number and called once or twice a week. He rambled on and on in a soothing voice about how we really needed to go out and how attractive I was. At some point, I stopped being scared. He said he had been in the Marines and now had a job at a farm management company. However, I thought he had lost interest in me when an entire summer passed with not a word from him. I dated a few guys from school, but everywhere we went I looked for Terry Wilson. He had put a spell on me; one I couldn't shake. Had he moved? Become interested in another girl?

A couple of weeks into October and another school year, I decided to spend the weekend with my parents. On Saturday evening, I made popcorn and turned on the television. Mary Tyler Moore's spunkiness and independence impressed me, but on this particular night, she came across as too sweet. The phone rang. I got there before my mother. It was Terry.

"Emilie, you're home, right? Let's get together next Saturday. I'll pick you up say around 7."

"You're askin' me to go out?" I wondered, but said it out loud.

"Yeah. Next Saturday. Be ready at 7. A buddy and I'll be out."

"Do you know where I live?"

"No problem. Got it. See you then?"

"I guess so," I answered not sure how the conversation had fallen into place. I wanted to be excited, but Mom, her usual nosey, overly-protective self, had been listening.

"It was him, right? Terry Wilson?" As if he were beneath us, scum. "Have you been seeing him? While you're at school?"

"No, Mom. Never. He asked me out, and I'm going…. I guess." I still couldn't believe how our short conversation had turned into a date. "Next Saturday."

"I don't approve. Your father won't approve. His reputation! And, what about yours? You don't know what you're getting yourself into." She started breathing heavily. I picked up the words *naïve, innocent*; but her phrases were no longer making sense. My father marched into the room, a look of vague defeat on his face.

"I'm eighteen-years-old. I'm a responsible person. Maybe he's a nice guy and no one's giving him a chance because of all the small-town gossipers." They both stared at me, looking helpless. I stood up, and said, "I'm going."

My parents looked distraught when I left the room—as if they had lost me—Dad was rubbing Mom's back while she wrung her hands and tried to control her breathing. I wanted to be excited. I had a date with a really cool, older guy. What would we do? Where would we hang out? I took a long look at myself in the full length mirror in my room after fleeing up the steps. Running my fingers through my hair, standing tall and throwing my shoulders back, I liked what I saw. Opening the closet door, I surveyed my wardrobe and wondered what I would wear.

I had difficulty concentrating on my classes and had trouble sleeping the following week in my dorm room. There were nightmares. Running barefoot through a thicket of thorny brambles, I discovered my clothes were in shreds and my arms and legs scratched and bruised. I awoke around 1:30 a.m., weeping uncontrollably, soaked in sweat, my pulse out of control. I questioned myself as to whether I should go through with this. *What would it hurt?* I asked myself. *It's just one date.* Everyone has an occasional nightmare, right?

I drove home after classes on Friday with a sinking feeling one moment and singing with Diana Ross on the radio the next, ... *ain't no mountain high enough, ain't no river wild enough to keep me from lovin' you.* I hummed the song as I unpacked a few of my belongings, did my laundry, and searched the kitchen cupboard for snacks. I used the excuse that I needed to study so that I could stay in my room and went to bed early, not wanting to get into arguments with my parents about me seeing Terry Wilson. Around 1:30, I woke up and could not get back to sleep. Even though it was mid-October, I opened the window wide and studied the sky. A moving star progressed steadily from one horizon to the other. A jet plane. And, I wondered what David was doing.

Breakfast was quiet that Saturday morning; my mom's rubbery fried eggs, limp toast, and cold orange juice stuck in my throat. Mom sat, her back straight, half-heartedly humming her usual hymn, "Blessed Assurance," and tapping her fingers on the side of a cold cup of coffee. Dad intermittently cleared his throat and moved his breakfast from one side of his plate to the other. Attempting to placate them, I asked Mom a question.

"What are the words to your song, all of them?" I asked her. She jumped in her chair.

"What do you mean?" she asked.

"Your song. You so often hum it. I know it's from church. I can't place it. Do you remember the words?"

"Well, of course, I do," she answered acting a little miffed, not the reaction I wanted. Dad pushed his chair back and left his breakfast on the table to do the morning chores. I waited.

"I'd like to hear them," I said. She softened a bit and started to sing.

"Blessed assurance, Jesus is mine. Oh, what a foretaste of glory divine. Heir of salvation, purchase of God, born of His Spirit, washed in His blood."

"Is that it?" I asked. "There's more, right?"

She swallowed once, twice, and offered a weak smile before continuing. Louder this time.

"This is my story; this is my song, praising my Savior all the day long. This is my Savior; this is my song, praising my Savior all the day long."

I watched tears come to her eyes and realized how precious her faith was to her. As I scraped my breakfast scraps into the garbage bin, I heard phrases from the next verse as she continued to sing softly: *Perfect submission… angels descending… echoes of mercy… whispers of love.* Wiping my own tears with the back of my hand, I left the house and sat on the front steps. I was at a stage of life when I did not fit in anywhere. My home no longer felt like home. The nursing program involved more studying than I had ever done in my life, and the social life at junior college was dismal.

A little later, I pulled myself together and called Mary, a college friend, and asked if she wanted to go shopping. Thankfully, she agreed. I bought something new to wear on my date, a sweater set with a matching skirt. Mary and I talked, mostly about school and our classes in nursing, that is, until she pulled into our farm driveway.

"So, what is it you're doing tonight?" Mary asked. I considered ignoring the question.

"Terry Wilson, he called. It's no big deal." I answered.

"Can I ask why?" she asked.

"Are you asking me why it's no big deal or…?"

"You're my friend. I care about you. That's why I'm asking." She snapped.

"Everyone seems shook up about this guy, Terry Wilson," I said, exasperated. "It's one night of my life. Probably a first date, last date thing. It's not like I plan to marry him or anything." Mary looked at me and waited.

"Hey, I need a little excitement in my life," I said.

"You mean a shopping trip with me isn't enough?" She kidded. We both relaxed a little. She gave me a shoulder hug and left with, "See you next week in class. It will be back to the books."

The house was empty when I carried my few packages in. Mom had written a message on the kitchen chalk board that she was pulling vines in the garden. When Mary left, I noted Dad was in the corncrib probably getting ready to do afternoon chores. I pulled my new outfit out of the bag, took a bath, and carefully applied makeup. With a little sprucing up, my old shoes would have to do. I considered applying nail polish and decided against it; I could not trust the tremor in my hands. Soon, the aroma of goulash came up the stairs along with discreet conversations between my parents. I knew I had to face them before leaving that night so I left my bedroom, descended the steps, and walked out into the kitchen. I sat at my usual spot at the kitchen table. My mom passed the peas and bread and butter.

"You look nice," she said. I didn't expect a compliment.

"Thanks," I answered. "I know you're both worried, but you don't need to be. I'll let you know when I'm home."

"Your usual curfew is midnight," my dad reminded me.

Bristling, I chose my words carefully. "Yes, my curfew was midnight when I was living at home and in high school. When I'm away at school, I have no curfew. Like I said, I'll let you know when I get home." I carried my untouched supper to the sink and went upstairs to wait. Feeling like the disobedient child who needed to be reprimanded, I wondered if my fascination with Terry Wilson was worth it. I paced the linoleum floor and periodically checked the gravel road stretching in front of our farm.

Before I heard the car, I saw the dust roll away from the gravel road, into the ditches, and hover over our field filled with golden rows of corn. A big, beefy, older Oldsmobile pulled into our farmstead. Two men sat in the front seat. I stared out the window and wondered why Terry came with someone else. Were we double dating? Not wanting a scene with my parents, I ran down the stairs, grabbed my coat and purse from the closet, and escaped out the back door. I met him as he was opening the front gate. Our eyes connected for the third time. Neither of us looked away for a few seconds. Then, Terry Wilson gave me a once over—you know, top to bottom look. I blushed; I hoped my parents weren't watching.

"Hi, I'm Emilie," I said and felt foolish. There had been telephone conversations with each other; eye contact from a distance, and here I was scooting into the backseat of a car with a guy who was a stranger. Should I sit in the middle? Should I sit next to the door? Terry climbed in before

I could decide and slid next to me, our thighs touching. Noting his light-colored Levi pants, a little too tight, I pulled my skirt over my knees. As we drove away, I turned to look at the farmhouse and the kitchen window framing my parents' faces. It would be my final memory of them.

———— ·❖❖❖· ————

# 4

Red flags? They were just that when I was growing up: flags. We placed them on the back of our bikes attached to a bendable pole and watched them whip in the wind. On the Fourth of July, we mixed the red with white and blue and went to the town parade. Even if someone had explained to me what a *red flag* was I would have missed it. If you're not looking for something, you're not going to see it.

Terry introduced me to our driver, Roger, his roommate, and I eventually realized that Roger and Terry lived in Terry's mother's house. The smell of men's cologne filled the car, and Terry was looking good. I recalled my first impression of him as he sat at the back of the auditorium during the Miss County Queen competition, the zing I felt.

"Just got out of the shower," he explained and ran his fingers through damp, light brown hair. I turned to look at him and our eyes locked again. The dark blue of his shirt magnified the intenseness in his cobalt eyes.

"Hey, girl, you are lookin' good," he whispered, our faces inches apart. Was it mouth wash or liquor on his breath? I felt awkward with his closeness and was relieved when Roger broke the spell.

"Hey, Terry, your ma told me you been gettin' death threats over the CB," Roger said, the corner of his mouth twitching while he eyed me in the rearview mirror.

"Yeah, don't make a big deal out of it, Roj," Terry replied, whacked the back of Roger's head, and placed his arm across my shoulders.

"Where are we going?" I asked. Roger fiddled with the radio, trying different stations as the miles rolled by. I was headed farther and farther from my parents with two men I knew virtually nothing about.

"Yeah, where are we going Roger?" Terry asked, with a note of mockery.

Roger ignored the question and started singing, "American Pie," with the radio. ... *bad news on the doorstep... something touched me deep inside... them good ole boys drinking whiskey and rye singin' this'll be the day that I die... and do you have faith in God above? ... Bye, bye Miss American Pie...*

"Roger!" Terry yelled. "Miss American Pie wants to know where we're goin'."

Roger continued to ignore Terry's question. Terry kissed the back of my hand.

"He's the driver. We'll let him decide," Terry stated. "Just relax, Baby," he murmured. "Known Roj a long time; he usually knows what he's doin'."

Roger eventually turned off the radio and began to talk. "Where do you go to school, Emilie?"

"The Junior College," I replied. "I'm in the nursing program." I was tired of sitting in the car, tired of the closeness of both of them.

"Impressive," he replied. "I thought about college. That's as far as I got. Thinking about it." He laughed. "Now, Terry, here, he joined the Marines!"

"Really? Wow!" I exclaimed although I already knew. "That's kind of a big deal, right?"

"Didn't last," Terry said. "Not my thing."

"Didn't fit in there, either, did ya?" Roger snorted and smacked the steering wheel a couple of times. I couldn't get a handle on Roger. He was either loud and sarcastic or quiet in a remorseful way.

"Bunch of jarheads taking orders from a sadistic drill sergeant," Terry responded.

"Couldn't take it, more like it, Buddy," Roger stated, matter-of-factly.

I didn't know how to participate in their conversation and was glad we had pulled into a parking lot. A neon sign blinked, "The Hut." People mingled outside.

"Hey, far out," Roger said, excited. "Gotta crowd already."

"Nice wheels, Roj," someone shouted as we got out of the Oldsmobile.

"Yeah, don't be a spaz," Roger replied. "They get me where I need to go." We kept walking towards the entrance, Terry's hand on my lower back. I heard Terry's name murmured within the group.

"Hey, Terry, what's the skinny on your new girl?" Some guy shouted, his fingers hooked in his leather jacket.

"Dream on," Terry replied and pulled me close.

"Yeah, you the man, Wilson; you the man," another chirped in.

Inside the The Hut, we had a beer at the bar. I pictured my parents' disapproval with every sip and drained the bottle. The juke box played Jimi Hendrix and Aerosmith. Heavy drums, aggressive beats rocked my brain, and I was almost relieved when we huddled back in the car. Again, Terry placed his arm across my shoulders with his left arm. He picked up my hand with his other arm. Beginning to feel claustrophobic, I withdrew my hand and pushed my hair off my forehead. It grew dark, telephone poles rushed by.

The sign, *Chester, Population 75*, popped up alongside the highway, and Roger whipped the car into a parking spot right in front of Harry's Lounge. Wherever we were, people knew Terry Wilson; but, other than his roommate, Roger, he never introduced me to anybody. Through various conversations, I tried to determine names and connections; however, tattered bits became meaningless, confusing. I felt clueless, out of my league. An eerie sense of something off-kilter hung in the air by a thread.

We went to Rocky's, another bar; the group was growing. The same people seemed to be showing up from bar to bar. Terry ordered hamburgers and asked if I had cash; he was running out. I handed him a twenty dollar bill, and he placed another drink in front of me. I wasn't used to drinking, but it gave me something to do; lousy excuse, I know. I stopped trying to make conversation and became the silent partner. Terry and I sat together in a booth, but he turned his body away from me, more interested in who was coming and going. I excused myself to use the restroom and stayed as long as I dared until a commotion erupted in the bar.

"Ya know ya got it, Wilson. You took it right off my truck, you thief!" A woman screamed. I left the bathroom to see her face within inches of Terry's. Tattooed arms, various piercings, and heavy makeup made it difficult to know if she was old or young.

"You're a fool. Shut up, Big Mouth! You ain't got nothin' on me." Terry yelled and turned away when he saw me, embarrassed. The woman continued swearing and threatened to blow away a certain part of his anatomy if he didn't return a radio and tapes.

"Are you okay?" I asked and wished I was home with my parents. Some men pulled the belligerent woman outside to cool off as she continued to thrash about.

"You mean, Star?" Terry chuckled, but I could tell he was shook up. "She makes a lot of noise. She ain't gonna hurt me. ... or blow away anything. No worries, Emilie." He laughed, a small laugh, smiled, and gave me a kiss on the cheek. It was the first time that night that he called me by name.

*I can do this*, I thought. I can get through the night and find something good about this guy. Prove my parents wrong. I took his hand in both of mine and studied his face. Light brown hair, sideburns, good tan, blue eyes. Seeing fine lines surrounding his eyes and both sides of his chin, I thought of him for the first time as *old*. His voice no longer sent me into emotional over-drive, and I had to admit that I just wanted to make it through the night and be a wiser, less naïve person come morning. I remembered what I had said earlier that day to Mary, *first date, last date....*

I was in the Marine Core, a Private," he said interrupting my thoughts.

"Really?" I knew this but encouraged him. "And what does a Private do?"

"What…" he asked. His mind was elsewhere.

"A Private in the Marine Corps," I reminded him. "What does that mean?"

"Entry-level rank, basic training kind of stuff. Found out it wasn't for me."

"So, you came home…"

"*Semper Fidelis*, it's the official motto of the Marines. *Always faithful* kind of stuff," he said. "Not for me."

I saw something in his eyes—a lost boy kind of look, but what did I know of life at eighteen? A recruiting poster displayed at college noted that the Marines are known for winning our nation's battles swiftly and aggressively in times of crisis. Terry Wilson didn't seem capable.

He held my hand as we got into the car and headed out of town. I didn't ask where we were going. The scent of men's cologne no longer filled the car, now replaced by a mingling of sweat, beer, smoke, fried food. After a short ride on country roads, we arrived to a farmhouse, draped by trees, and needing paint. Other cars were parked helter-skelter under a dim pole light in the farm yard. Someone met us at a side door tucked in between overgrown bushes. He and Terry exchanged talk about work before he acknowledged me.

"New girl? Where's the other gal? Susie, the high school chick?" He chided as we stepped onto the front porch. Terry avoided the question and pulled me into the farmhouse. "Probably scared her away with all that talk about you being afraid of getting shot at," he mumbled. Terry said nothing.

In the living room, there were no couch spaces or empty chairs left. The movie, *Tick, Tick, Tick*— started on late-night television. A pistol in the left hand corner and a sheriff standing in front of a squad car filled the screen. Someone opened a cooler and passed out beers. Terry and I lay on the floor in front of the television. I slipped my shoes off and pulled my skirt down, feeling self-conscious around this crowd who all seemed to know each other although did not necessarily *like* each other. The overhead light was off; a lamp lit a corner of the room. Jim Brown, George Kennedy and Fredric March played roles in a racially torn Southern town. The movie held my attention. Part way through, Hank Williams, Jr., sang "A Time to Sing"... and certain phrases seemed to connect with Terry. *The waters of a river flow down stream...But no man ever knows what his life will bring...*

Terry, watery eyed, chewed a fingernail and stared at the TV. Car lights traced the ceiling; a horn blasted; a car door slammed.

"Hey, Wilson, get out here! It's the Wicked Witch," someone yelled from the kitchen. Terry jumped up, a smirk on his face.

"Stay here," he said to me. "Watch the movie." I returned to the carpeted floor and sat on my knees. Someone turned the volume down on the TV. One by one, everyone ventured to the picture window adjacent to the driveway. I followed and tapped someone's shoulder in front of me.

"Who is she? The Wicked Witch?" I asked. I stood on my tiptoes to see; it looked like the tattooed woman who had threatened Terry earlier.

"You mean, Star?" she asked. "Thinks she's tough because she's a truck driver. Has a big mouth, that's about it." I watched Terry and Star under the yard light as another car pulled into the drive and parked under a cluster of trees. A couple got out, stayed in the shadows, and watched from a distance. The girl beside me muttered, "Howard and Linda Black. What a time to show up."

Every time Terry made a move to get back in the house, Star blocked him, her arms extended. She was just as tall as Terry and probably outweighed him by twenty pounds. A few quiet words were exchanged before

KATHLEEN STAUFFER

Terry wrapped his arms around her in a bear hug and kissed her—long and hard. Whoops and howls erupted inside the house.

*Tick, Tick, Tick* played out behind me. Feeling a sense of abandonment, I no longer cared about the movie or Terry Wilson and hoped I would never again see anyone gathered in this house. Following backslaps from his so-called buddies, Terry came back to the place on the floor, a grin on his face. The others returned to their chairs and places on the couch. I stayed on my knees, hands folded on my lap, and tried to regulate my breathing. Looking about the room, I recognized the last couple to arrive, the couple who had lingered in the shadows under the trees during the argument. Howard and Linda Black had joined the bar-hopping group at some point. They remained in the doorway between the kitchen and living room, checking out the group and acting unsure if they were going to stay. My thoughts were interrupted by hoarse whispers coming from the kitchen.

"Get these guys out of here…." A female voice hissed. "You're askin' for trouble!" A few stirred in their seats but returned to focus on the conclusion of the movie.

"Movie's almost over," a guy answered harshly. "They'll be out of here. You're over reactin'. Don't make a big deal of it."

The burger I had eaten, the alcohol, the tension, and tiredness made me queasy. I considered going outside for fresh air, wondered how far away I was from home, and if I started walking, would I be able to get there…. I did not want to be here. I checked my watch. It was 1:00 a.m. I knew my parents would be worried. I wanted to ask Terry to take me home, but he seemed to be counting on everyone else for transportation. I felt trapped. *Tick, Tick, Tick* credits rolled on the screen. A commentator broke the silence in the room with, "This concludes another day of television broadcasting. Good night and good morning." The National Anthem played with a flag unfurling. Static filled the screen.

"I should get home," I whispered to Terry.

Coats and keys were gathered. A few beer bottles clunked and then rolled across the floor. Eerie quiet spilled out of the house along with everyone's footsteps. Something was vaguely disturbing. There were no *good-nights*, no *thank you's* for the hospitality as everyone headed to their cars. Terry and I walked with our heads down, no longer touching or holding hands. Two sets of feet appeared on the ground before us blocking our progress. We stopped and looked up.

"Need a ride?" Howard Black asked Terry. Howard's wife, Linda, clung to his side, her glasses on the tip of her nose, her hair strewn. Terry, hands in his Levi's, watched the other cars pull from the farmstead, one by one. Roj, his roommate, and the big Oldsmobile were nowhere in sight. Terry nodded a yes, placed his hand on my lower back and guided me to the only car left.

"You drive," Howard said and handed Terry his keys. "We'll take the back. Gotta take your girl home, right?"

I opened the front car door on my own and slid onto the cold vinyl seat. I yearned to be asleep on my lumpy mattress in my bedroom with the slanted ceilings, raindrops pelting the roof. The others got into the car. The doors closed, one by one. Linda sat behind me; Howard sat behind Terry. It was so quiet, I could hear my heart beat and sensed that someone else climbed into the back seat; however, I didn't know anyone anyway and didn't care. Terry started the car; overhead tree branches scraped the roof as we left the farmstead and then pulled onto the county road. Seeing the road sign, County Road B, I couldn't help but remember Michael, the teenager, a hit and run victim who had died on this same road not so long ago, still a cold case, never resolved. I wrapped myself in my tweed coat, clutched my purse, and let my thoughts drift. I thought of Pastor Snider and his explanation of evil.

According to Pastor Snider, evil was not a part of God's original creation. There was a war in heaven because Satan was not content to be a servant of God. Satan left and ventured to Eden where he lured Eve. I imagined the conversation with Adam after Eve took that infamous bite.

"Why did you do that, Eve?" Adam scolded. "You know that God forbade us to eat of that tree. How could you have been so stupid?"

The word *stupid* pierced Eve's heart. Adam had never spoken to her this way. Defensively, she replied, "You took a bite! You're just as guilty as I am."

Tired of my own creative thoughts, I made myself small and closed my eyes, heavy with sleep and too much to drink, not noticing the quiver in Terry's hands as he clutched the steering wheel.

———————— ✦✦✦✦✦ ————————

My recollections from this point are nebulous, vague, other-worldly. Yes, I saw things; I heard things. I was there.

Then, I was not.

There were harsh words; car doors opened and slammed shut; cold air crept in. The car became empty, except for me. Had I drifted off to sleep? The car's headlights penetrated the black county highway exposing two shadowy figures—one threatening; the other pleading. Scuffling followed; the car shook. A bang echoed. Then another, and I prayed hysterically, *Dear God in heaven... Help me. Thy kingdom come, thy will be done....and forgive us ...Oh, God, help me.*

A shadow passed my side of the car. Panicky, I moved to lock the door—too late. It sprang open; someone grabbed my hair, and twisted my head backwards.

"Terry!" I screamed. Unable to get my balance, unable to stand, I tumbled onto the ground, arms flailing, heart hammering out of control. Heavy breathing, curse words, and the smell of sweat enclosed me. "Terry?!" Were there two arms, four? Gravel grit filled my mouth; someone's knees were on my back. Cold, injured, and terrified, I recalled my parents' pale faces framed by the kitchen window and sobbed, my chest on fire.

The now familiar nightmare came at me in flashes: reddish spatters, running through brambles and branches, shredded clothing. The moon grew cold. A falling star. And then, reality: Thud. Thud. Thud.... My heart exploded. Hot pain. *Jesus....*

———————— ✦✦✦✦✦ ————————

# 5

*With the LORD a day is like a thousand years and a thousand years are like a day.* A car departed the scene; tail lights grew dim, floated down the road—leaving a scent of dust and death. In the near distance, a dog barked frantically. The wind whipped a few straggling trees growing in a fence line. I heard the sound of it, but I did not know where it came from or where it went. My face felt damp. I was on the fringe of nothingness. I was on the fringe of everything.

Soon, a single car light from another direction loomed in the thickness, one of its headlights missing. It came near; its wheels drove through a puddle of darkness. Some of it spattered on my shoes, on my coat and purse. But I no longer had need for them. Terry lay on the other side of the road. I wanted to help him, but he had no need for my help. In the wee-wee hours of dawning, another car emerged. A man dressed in hunting clothes, his eyes focused on the road. I wanted to stop him and ask for help, but there was no need for help anymore. I regarded the pretty girl on the ground, swollen and discolored face, battered and tattered body, lying in a pool of oblivion, her eyes dwelling on dwindling stars.

Time passed. Quickly or slowly, I could not tell. The puddle was becoming a dark stain. Tall ditch grass, weeds, our dark clothing blended with earth's colors and time of day. A couple more cars drove by, as if nothing, absolutely nothing, had happened, and I wondered what world I was in. Fishermen from Big Stone Lake? Duck hunters? My mom was an early riser; she would soon be pulling the pots and pans out to fix Dad's breakfast of eggs, bacon, toast, and coffee. They would be worried....

When little, there were fears: the big bad wolf, a nail in the foot requiring a tetanus shot, being chosen last for a game. In nursing school, the fears matured with me: a test with 500 questions, the first time I administered an inoculation to a real person. But you see no one can hurt me anymore, and I'll never finish nursing school. Earthly feelings were scattered in the fields of corn and beans; gut instincts took flight with a chilling breeze; previous influences departed. I am free and yet I am not.

A piercing chirp catches my attention. A brilliant red bird sits on the County Road B 20 signpost surveying the situation. And then an additional sound—the rumble of yet another car approaching. A grizzled farmer dressed in chore clothes, much like my dad wore, driving a new Pontiac. I recognize Joseph Turner, an elder in our church. He pays no attention to my lifeless body in the early morning gloom or the sticky puddle in the middle of the road—his thoughts elsewhere. The right blinker kicks in, and the Pontiac turns into a farm drive several miles down the road. It is his brother, Jacob's house. A dog barks; the bird chirps repeatedly.

I contemplated things I've never considered before... Am I here because I long for justice? I wonder and, yet, it does not weigh on my soul as you might think. I have angry, bitter, or revengeful moments. But they are brief flashes, and I have found that grace is surrounding me, protecting me, humbling me.

I'm still me, not a Siamese cat slinking about, not an Eagle soaring above some cliff. I don't believe in reincarnation. In fact, I'm more *me* than you are *you*. And, I am not an angel. God created angels to be angels. I am not one of them. I can't see inside a person's head nor will anyone feel my presence. I've landed in another spot—a place where my heart and soul have been shifted—waiting for an end that feels finished.

I watch Joseph get out of his car unaware of what he passed through a few miles back. He heads for the machine shed where farm equipment is stored that he and his brother share. Considering the weather, how many acres could be harvested this day, and the number of potential bushels of corn they would be delivering to the elevator for storage, he unhooks the latch and slides the door back that opens the shed. I follow and yearn for something to happen.

————— ⋅⋅✦✦✦⋅⋅ —————

# 6

Joseph Turner had experienced enough in his time to understand that life was not meant to be easy. He didn't expect it to be. After World War II, he returned home to start a family and farm. There were pigs, steers, and chickens to be fed. Grain needed to be ground, bales needed to be moved, pens for the various animals needed to be cleaned. Plowing, planting, and harvesting were all seasonal tasks. The Turner children were expected to help raise their younger siblings and assist in whatever way they could with endless chores. There were ragweed, thistles, and foxtail to be pulled in the corn and bean fields; chickens to be butchered and dressed; eggs to be gathered; and cows to be milked. Joseph was up before daybreak and rested long after the sun went down. He was a task-master, made daily lists, and yet knew how to have fun.

He was also competitive. With no television in the house, family softball games were prevalent on summer days after a meal. Dishes were cleared; everyone yelled "first bat." Whoever got out of the house and to home plate first got the honors, despite a little pushing and shoving. Irene, his wife, also participated and was a worthy slugger, but became so tickled she could not get around the bases without getting out. There were board games on Sundays. He served as the in-house math tutor; Irene helped her children with spelling and literature.

Losing a twenty-two year old son in a plane crash was devastating. The ups and downs of raising five girls, maintaining the work and financial load of a farm, and community responsibilities took its toll. He was a respected board member of the Farmers' Elevator, St. Paul's Nursing Home, and his church. He and Irene took the Bethel Bible classes and had verses written on notes taped on mirrors, windows, and various cabinets throughout their farmhouse. When brushing their teeth, making supper, or getting ready to do chores, they worked on their memory work. After sitting down for breakfast each morning, they recited together Psalm 121, *I will lift my eyes to the mountains, from whence cometh my help. My help cometh from the LORD...* Joseph and Irene persisted with a faith in God that was beyond measure.

Planting, watching the seedlings sprout, and praying for the just-right amounts of rain and sunshine to provide an abundant harvest was his life. It was corn picking time, October, a cold and dreary day. Joseph arose that Saturday, scrambled a few eggs, and ate hurriedly. The house was quiet. The girls were grown-up, married, and on their own. Irene was away helping one of them who recently had surgery. Wanting to get to his brother's house before sunrise, he filled a thermos with steaming coffee and headed for the backdoor where his insulated coveralls and overshoes waited for him.

Joseph Turner's footprints were all over the farmyard, from corncrib to tool shed, from tool shed to the barn, from the barn to the pig house and in and out of the fields. However, there weren't many chores to attend to anymore. An old barn was a roost for birds; the pig house no longer squealed with the arrival of piglets. The windmill spun overhead, and he remembered the children wanting to venture a climb in spite of his nay-saying. All seemed to be in order as he climbed into his brother's Pontiac to make the ten minute drive to Jacob's place where he had left the heavy harvesting equipment the night before.

Not wanting to bother Jacob, Joseph parked the Pontiac near the machine shed where the corn picker had already been hooked up and the mechanisms checked. Joseph settled in the tractor seat, put it in gear, and pulled out of the large shed on to County Road B 20. A gust sent shivers along his arms and legs, and he wondered if he had dressed warmly enough. Pulling on his gloves, he put the tractor in low and pulled away from his brother's farm. Scanning the ditches for pheasants from his higher position on the tractor, he was relieved the season would not open for a few days. The extra road traffic and the sound of guns rattled him. He looked forward to the hum-drum of a corn picker sweeping the fields clean and the occasional break at the end of the rows for a hot cup of coffee from his thermos.

A mile or more down the road, Joseph noticed a large lump in the ditch and pumped the brake and clutch on the tractor for a better look. A man's body, his face and hands already gray, lay crumpled, surrounded by weeds. He scanned the fields, row after row of corn—ready for a harvest—wondering what they hid. His eyes moved from one horizon to another. Knowing he could not handle this alone, he put the giant contraption in gear and went to the end of the mile where he made a U-turn, tractor along with corn picker, to return to Jacob's farm. As he neared the site of the body, he slowed to get a better look at the scene. To his horror, he saw another body on the opposite side of the road, that of a young woman, lying in a field driveway. Her coat was stripped from one side of her body; a purse and one shoe were a few feet from her. He looked from one corpse to another; his mind went blank. Cold air slithering down his back and up his coat sleeves brought him back to reality. He turned in one direction and then the other; he twisted and looked behind him, the tractor seat moaning beneath him with every move. Were there more bodies? Was some insane person hiding in the fields intending even more harm? How had this happened? Who would do such a horrible thing? And why here?

A raw, metallic chirping penetrated the early morning. Joseph spotted a cardinal, brilliant in color, sitting on a fence post nearby, as if protecting his turf. *Unusual*, Joseph thought. But, these were not usual circumstances.

Not sure if he could keep the tractor on the road, he thought about walking back to his brother's farm. But, he had no strength to do so. His legs were wobbly and unpredictable along with his mental state. Seeing the horror of two dead bodies, Joseph felt exposed, in danger himself. Again, he put the tractor in gear and drove back to Jacob's at a snail's pace; he could not trust himself to do it any other way.

Joseph turned into his brother's farmstead and spotted Jacob in the garage getting ready for his own work day. Jacob hooked his fingers in his overalls and wondered what his older brother was up to. Out of gas? Something wrong with the picker? Joseph parked the huge implement in front of the garage and climbed down cautiously, his hands clutching each hold as Jacob watched.

"What is it, Joseph? You're as white as a sheet."

"May God have mercy...." Joseph breathed, his voice hoarse, barely above a whisper.

"Joseph! What is it? Are you okay?"

"God have mercy...we gotta get help. Something really bad happened."

Joseph removed his farm cap with earflaps and ran his hand through his thinning hair. "… bodies on the road."

"You, okay, Joseph? *You're* all right, right?"

"Get the car," Joseph said, and then added, "We need to be careful, Jacob; this is not good."

Puzzled, Jacob backed the car out of the garage, and the two brothers crept down the county road, the sound of gravel cracking. Jacob soon realized he had no first aid kit, no blanket to assist a victim in shock. He was totally unprepared. Thinking *car accident*, he had no way to prepare for what he was about to see. His brother beside him, shivered uncontrollably, and held his hands between his knees murmuring bits and pieces from scripture … *the LORD will give us strength, do not repay evil for evil, we need to be strong and courageous, He heals the broken hearted….*

"Joseph! You've got to tell me what's goin' on," Jacob prodded his brother as a dark stain appeared in the middle of the road. Jacob stopped the car, his eyes lingering on the smeared blotches spilled on the roadside.

"Did you hit a deer, Joseph?"

"No, no deer." Joseph was finally able to use words. He took a deep breath, "There's bodies in the ditch, both sides." Jacob rolled down his window and stretched high in his seat. A young girl's body lay in a lane dipping down into a corn field. A man's body lay across the road in a heap, his legs and arms twisted as if he had been rolled into the ditch.

"Good God, Joseph. What is this?"

Shaken, both men got out of the car and approached the ditch. A man, dressed in dirty Levis and a vinyl jacket, looked up at them, eyes partially closed, a bullet hole to the head. Although Halloween was just a week away, the brothers knew this was no prank. Jacob took a few steps into the deep ditch. He didn't want to stare, but he could not take his eyes off the bullet hole, black and deep, surrounded by red almost in the shape of a star. He scanned the fields, row after row of corn—ready for a harvest—and wondered what they hid. A cardinal's piercing chirp caused him to lose his balance. He landed on his back and started to slide on the slippery grass toward the gruesome figure.

"Jesus, the Christ," Jacob blurted. Joseph had never heard his brother use such words, except in church and in prayer. Under the circumstances,

Joseph absorbed it as a prayer and repeated his brother's words, *Jesus, the Christ, help us.*

Joseph offered his brother a hand as Jacob struggled from the ditch, their grips both cold and sweaty. Joseph held his brother's elbow as they walked around the by-now sticky puddle in the middle of the road and approached a young woman's body. Dressed in a matching sweater and skirt, her shoes and legs covered with embedded gravel and wet spatters, she faced the sky, a look of bewilderment and shock on her face. Although the Turner brothers were relieved this child was not one of theirs, their hearts were heavy for the family who surely knew nothing of this horrific crime.

––––––––– ⁑ –––––––––

Jacob's wife, Evelyn, looked from the kitchen window as her husband and brother-in-law turned into the driveway. Busy with peeling vegetables for a pot roast, she thought little of it. The Turner brothers had farmed together for years, shared equipment, and planned their spring planting and harvesting to be able to accomplish everything with shared machinery. Evidently, some problem had turned up. They would work it out; they always had. She watched as they both sauntered to the garage. Poker, their family border collie, barked sharply, sniffed at their heels, and started to howl. She recalled his barking during the early morning hours, untypical behavior for him. Neither Joseph nor Jacob was speaking; something seemed off-kilter; their faces were too serious. Clearing the sink of potato and carrot peals, she opened the cupboards to pull out the roasting pan. Meanwhile, Jacob had no idea how he would share such news with his wife or anyone else for that matter. However, he knew a phone call had to be made to the local sheriff. In the garage, an extra phone was attached to the unfinished framework of a wall. He dialed the sheriff's office and handed the receiver to his brother.

"Here, Joseph, you talk. You saw if first," Jacob said to his brother.

Shaking with every ring, Joseph's nerves became more frazzled.

"Remember the boy, Michael?" Jacob interjected.

"Hit and run," Joseph answered quietly. "More than a year ago. This is somethin' else, Jacob. This is...."

"County sheriff's office," a young female voice answered on the fifth ring.

"Yes." Joseph took several breaths not sure if he could speak. His brother sat beside him in an old lawn chair, head bent low. "There's two dead bodies out here, a little over a mile from the Jacob Turner farm." The girl said nothing. Jacob got up from the lawn chair, paced back and forth on the gravel outside the garage.

"Hello, did you hear me?" Joseph asked, impatient, louder than he intended.

"Yeah, County Sheriff, here," a curt male voice answered. "What's going on, sir?"

"There's two dead bodies on County Road B 20. One on either side of the road..."

"Pretty early in the morning to be drunk. We got better things to do than take prank calls," the sheriff cut in. Flabbergasted, Joseph handed the phone to his brother.

"Jacob Turner, here, if you know how to do your job, you'll get out here before I hang this phone up! There's two dead bodies with gunshot wounds!"

I watched them. I listened to the Turner brothers and felt sympathy for them. Of course, I remember Michael, the eighteen-year-old hit and run victim. The dog barking? Yes, that was Poker and no wonder he was frantic. Watching Evelyn in the kitchen reminded me of my own mother. Jacob and Joseph were terrified, frustrated, their lives forever changed as they headed back to the scene.

⋅⋅✦✦✦⋅⋅

# 7

Faint light, barely visible above the rows of corn, filtered on the horizon as the stars faded one by one and cars with official licenses hurried down the county road, sirens screaming. I struggled to remember where I was and how I had gotten there as each person got out of his car and crept close to the scene. Their gazes flickered from one side of the road to the other; their mouths were slightly parted; their eyes wide. The corn rustled, Jacob's dog yelped in the distance, the bird tweeted, and for a few heartbeats, no one spoke. A sense of dread hung over everything. The sheriff noted the Turner brothers down the road diverting traffic and felt a twinge of shame. Horrors they had never imagined lay before them.

Another vehicle rushed to the scene with a **Bureau of Criminal Investigation** placard fixed on the side of the car. I watched as bits and pieces were collected from the ditch, from the road; others scribbled notes on legal pads. The sun periodically stole glimpses between accumulating clouds. The county coroner hovered over me for a few minutes and distinctly pronounced me *dead*. And then moments later, he pronounced Terry Wilson *dead*. Two white, windowless vans drove at a measured pace on the county road and pulled up to the site. Emilie Fischer's body was placed on a stretcher and carried to one. Terry Wilson's body was placed on a stretcher and carried to another. Officials, dressed in stiff, uncomfortable uniforms, intermittently straggled back to their respective cars, their heads hanging, full of haunting images and a question—*Who would have done this?*

Curious, I followed the van with my lifeless body to a funeral home while a dispatcher headed gradually in his own car in another direction: someone had to deliver the news to Emilie Fischer's parents. I could not bear to see my parents' reactions. Instead, I situated myself in a large room where instruments and notepads were distributed among bright lights. During hushed conversations, I watched them pull a large wooden splinter from my hair. The coroner questioned his assistant *…from the gun grip?* Scribbled notes mentioned embedded gravel, a crushed skull, superficial facial abrasions; shots to my head, abdomen, and through my heart. *How did I live through this?* I wondered. And then reminded myself that I had not. There were more words and phrases about partially digested food— indicating an *agitated and nervous state* —and blood alcohol content, and I wondered why they needed to know so much.

*For My thoughts are not your thoughts neither are your ways My ways,* the words from Isaiah, hung in the air soon to be followed by a dream unspooling that I had had so long ago…. scrambling wildly through a grove of prickly undergrowth with thorny vines and brambles whipping my face. And, now, crimson stains my clothes and scarlet drops batter me like rain. I try to clear my eyes, but everything, everything is blurry.

"EMILIE!"

I tried opening my eyes. Nothing was working.

"EMILIE!"

"What…?" I answered. I could not determine where the deep voice was coming from.

"EMILIE, LISTEN CAREFULLY."

"Who are you?"

"I AM."

"Excuse me….?"

"OCCUPY THE TERRITORY ASSIGNED TO YOU."

"My territory?"

"YOU WILL NOT LIVE EFFECTIVELY ETERNALLY UNLESS YOU KNOW WHAT TO DO WITH YOUR YESTERDAYS."

"Eternally? Yesterday? But, I messed up. I messed up bad."

"SELF-CONDEMNATION DOES NOT HONOR GOD."

"God?"

"YOUR LIFE MAY BE A STRAND IN A BIGGER STORY."

"God???"

"YES, I AM."

Time shifted, bounced, shrank, echoed. *My thoughts are not your thoughts and my ways are not your ways.* My father's words on confirmation

Sunday crossed my brain like a banner, "There'll be a few bumps in the road, but God will get you where you need to go."

"*Really*, dear God? *Here?*" I implored.

I lingered on the edge of things and somewhere in the clouds. They had always fascinated me. As a child during stormy weather, I would leave the farmhouse and venture out into a lightening filled sky and wait for the rain to wash the sweat and grime from my summer childhood skin. Later, I would search for a rainbow and watch the clouds race to new horizons.

I could not stop thinking about clouds. I was in between having a thousand feelings and yet none at all.

"EMILIE?"

"Yes," I whispered, head bowed.

"BOOTS ON THE GROUND."

--------◆◆◆◆◆◆--------

# 8

The sun would rise; the sun would set; but from now on our small community and its surrounding area would view the world differently. A locality that thrived on routine realized that change, mystery, and fear would become the new normal. Speculation ran helter-skelter when the local newspaper came out with the headline, "First Date; Last Date," the day after the double homicide. *Why* and *Who* hung in the air, slipped from lips, and shadowed persons wherever they went in a blob of blue ink. Everyone locked their doors at night and some during the day for weeks and then months. Parents kept their children inside. When anyone heard the sound of an approaching car, eyes peeked from windows to see—neighbor or stranger? Driving at night was frightening. Some events were postponed.

*What kind of monster could have done this? Who was he? Where was he?* ...was fodder for on-going conversations. However, when an eighteen-year-old girl goes out with a thirty-year-old man, there's even more. Unproven details, scandalous tidbits, busy bodies firing hearsay, the local papers kept it going by printing comments.

*How terrible—murdered on their first date.*

*Eighteen and going out with a thirty year old man with kids—possibly illegitimate?*

*Who are these people and do we still need to be afraid?*

*I pray justice is served. I pray for the families.*

*God will get them.*

Where the gossipers came up with illegitimate children, I know not. Remember, I have a problem with that word. The granite stone belonging to Terry Wilson in the cemetery mentions no *father of, loved by*. There is a small cross within a circle above his name. His father and a brother were at Terry's funeral, standing shoulder to shoulder in their worn-out black suits, scuffs on their shoes, haggard faces. Within two years, Terry Wilson's father and brother would be lying on either side of Terry's grave. Why is it that in some families, tragedy becomes too common? Who can understand….

**Charge Howard and Linda Black with Murder** were headlines of the day on November 15, 1976, in our local paper. **Blacks Plead Not Guilty** followed a few days later with a picture of a twenty-five-year-old man brushing black, shaggy bangs from his face, confidence in his eyes; his wife, much shorter, followed behind, head bowed.

**Saints Football Loses the Battle in Class A Championship Game** also made the front page along with postal guidelines for Christmas gift-sending. But, overall, the coming holidays and football took the backburner in the weeks and months to come. Murder on a country road wasn't an everyday occurrence.

Determining that it would be difficult to get a fair and impartial jury close to home, the trial location was moved from one county to another. Moving a double homicide trial forty-five minutes away is not going to give you a more objective jury, especially since the story and my Miss County Queen competition picture made MURDER MYSTERIES, an American crime series magazine. An entire part of our state felt on the verge of something deplorable and explosive. Neighbors and classmates were popping up their heads like groundhogs reading the paper for the first time and talking to people they had never talked to with questions like, *What really happened? Who did this? Why? Why?*

I watched all this, experienced it in a way no one else could and had a lot of think time. I have determined that God is okay with questions. There are over 3000 questions in the Bible. The book of Job has the most. Job's so-called *friends* do most of the asking. Job's livestock, children, and servants were destroyed, and then he is afflicted with painful sores from the soles of his feet to the top of his head. Could the situation get worse? His friends' questions are not comforting. They are more of the type as to *what did you do to deserve this, Job?* Believe me, I get it; I have no doubt that some of my friends are asking the same questions about me, as in *What did you do to deserve this, Emilie Fischer?* Well, thankfully, God has questions of his own, *Where were you when I laid the earth's foundation? Who shut up the sea behind doors? Have you ever given orders to the morning, or shown the dawn its place?* Kind of puts things in perspective, don't you think?

Those connected to the homicides and a curious assortment of others rose early that first day of trial and lined up outside the court house like hungry piranhas waiting for a handout. I hung out in the shade of a nearby evergreen, inquisitive myself. Let me see, Mrs. Stewart surely cancelled her piano students' lessons for the day to be here. The Johnson sisters relinquished their usual coffee date. Mr. Hewett, the school custodian, took a vacation day. I saw my parents, faces downcast, and David standing beside them and wondered what he gave up to be here and why. I wanted to go to them, ease their pain, but there are no do-overs in life, and I cannot take this away from anyone.

When the doors opened, everyone hushed. A pesky cardinal harkened above; no one paid attention. Grumbling began however when some were turned away; all seats had been taken. After the door clicked shut, I slipped in and surveyed the surroundings. Two prosecuting attorneys sat alone at one table near the jury panel. Three defending attorneys along with Howard and Linda Black sat at another table. A court reporter sat between the judge's bench and the witness chair. The court bailiff sat among forty some spectators, including media experts and a sketch artist. I wandered from the prosecutor's table to the defense table and tried looking over their shoulders at legal pads filled with handwritten notes. There were minutes when I would study the jurors, seven men and five women, ordinary people given an extraordinary task, and try to determine what they were thinking.

A swarm of inquisitive seekers filled the seats every day. I found them interesting and at times amusing. A mother dragged her twelve year old son into court with, "You're going to thank me someday. It's not every day you get to see a murder trial." During lunch, they would go in shifts and save places for each other—not wanting to miss out on anything. I could only imagine the tidbits that filled their worldly brains that they carried with them at the end of the day.

Interested myself, I remained in and around the building and learned some history by reading various inscriptions. Destroyed by fire in 1872, over one hundred years ago by your time table, a new courthouse was eventually completed by 1891. Its massive structure, with tower-like turrets, surveyed a multitude of manicured trees and shrubs on the courthouse lawn. Besides reading about the history of the court house, I observed birds and butterflies, and especially a red cardinal who seemed to be just as nosy as everyone else.

Days and weeks passed. I counted a total of eighty-five witnesses who testified... *It gave me something to do...* sharing more information than I could wrap my mind around. The majority of the witnesses, however, were local— including Terry's family and mine and his so-called friends, most of whom were at the gathering at the farmhouse watching the movie, *Tick, Tick, Tick*. And, of course, there were the Turner brothers, Joseph and Jacob.

Joseph was the first to testify. Dressed in his Sunday suit and tie, he answered questions about discovering the bodies, the time, the place. He was confident but I could tell he would rather be at home, on the farm, doing his chores, taking care of business rather than wrapped up in this mess someone else had created.

The same old nightmare puzzled me at unpredictable times. Running through brambles, bushes, thorns, crimson spots, blurry vision. Running away from someone or running to something? I couldn't make sense of it and wondered why the vision kept pestering me. Testimonies came at me like tumultuous waves with hundreds of things to consider. I did not understand how any of this could be connected to *my* murder. At times it seemed insignificant, meaningless, boring.

I felt emotional retching when my friend, Mary, told of a call from my dad around 1:30 a.m., October 23, explaining that I had not returned home. And asking, *Would you please go look for Emilie? Her mother and I are worried.* My parents were in the court room every day of the trial where their child, Emilie Fischer, had become a degrading display of evidence. I sat between them at times and held both of their hands, but I could no longer comfort them.

I did not know the majority of the witnesses; however, I remembered Star. She intrigued me; she was dressed up, probably wearing the best she had. A truck driver with a flamboyant personality, ostentatious behavior, and a big mouth; she was the only witness who sobbed when she declared, "I did not kill Terry Wilson." What lies beneath that tough exterior only God knows.

I watched her walk uneasily back to her seat in a too-tight dress and high heels and then directed my attention back to the witness stand as they summoned Howard Lee Black. Howard had given his keys to Terry so that I had a ride home. Howard and his wife, Linda, sat in the backseat as we left the farmstead. I remember feeling miserable, wrapping my arms around myself, being drowsy and wondering if there were only two in the backseat or were there three? I only wanted to be home.

Howard's hair rested on his shirt collar. He leaned slightly forward in the witness stand, face pale, hands on his knees, stroking his mustache. There were questions about his various jobs, his attempts as a college student, and his current employment as a custodian. The prosecution peppered him with questions about that night two people were murdered on a county road. He denied killing Terry Wilson. He denied killing Emilie Fischer.

I screamed out the word *liar*. Everyone else could have heard a pin drop.

Linda Black, Howard's wife, the young woman who sat behind my seat in the car that night, followed her husband as the next witness. I paid special attention to her. Her indifferent expression was hidden by her long, drab hair and large-framed glasses which she kept adjusting. With arms crossed, I approached the witness stand as Linda explained that she knew Terry Wilson *from the bars*, as she put it. I was spellbound when she admitted, after further questioning by the prosecution, that she and Terry once lived together. I propped my elbows on the rail surrounding the witness' chair, inches from her face, when the prosecution gently asked, "Linda, do you have children?"

"What do you mean?" she answered, tears immediately filling her eyes.

"Objection!" The Black's attorney yelled.

"Over-ruled," the judge replied and nodded to the prosecutor.

"It's not a difficult question, Mrs. Black. Is it not true that you have a deceased child?"

Linda took the tissues offered and blew her nose. Sitting up straight and finding her husband's eyes, she asked, "What does that have to do with anything?"

"May I remind you, Mrs. Black, that you are under oath and can be found in contempt of court." The prosecuting attorney stares briefly at her and looks at the jury before asking, "Would you like me to repeat the question, is it true that….?"

"Yes. Sammy, I called him," Linda Black stated matter-of-factly. "His name was Samuel. He was only two years old." By this time, Linda's nose was running and tears were streaming. The prosecuting attorney offered her another tissue.

"Our sympathies, Mrs. Black." He waited. "Can you tell us what happened to Sammy?"

"What do you mean what *happened*?" Linda retorted, anger emerging.

"The cause of death?"

"It was an accident," she said and sat up straighter.

"Were you with Sammy when he died?"

"No! I was not."

"Who was taking care of Sammy when the accident occurred?"

Linda looked at the jury for the first time and replied, "Terry Wilson."

Spectators gasped; a few jury members murmured. The judge pounded his gavel and asked for order. I wandered outside, emotional and confused, and wondering *what does this have to do with me?* At the same time, I considered a mother's pain when losing a child so young.

When I returned, two other women, supposed confidants of Linda, testified that Linda Black had shared private conversations implying, *If my child can't live, then neither can Terry Wilson.* A motive for murder? I recalled hearing that the state does not have to give evidence of a motive for the alleged crime; rather, they only need evidence that the crime was committed.

I wondered where Samuel was, his burial site… I got lost in my thoughts when another woman took the stand, Leslie Ray Wilson. Leslie was *married*, but separated from Terry at the time of his death. Leslie was out of town the night he was murdered. Terry's *wife* was out of town on the night of our first date, last date? …my mind tumbled back to the many hours I had spent with a man I knew nothing of. Although I felt sucker-punched, I folded my hands and sent a prayer to our God above for these women.

I yearned to talk to my parents—to tell them they were right to be afraid for me. I yearned to tell David I was sorry for what we could have had. I wanted to scream to the jury, *The Blacks did this! They had a reason!*

I would be angry too if someone hurt my child, if someone else killed my child because of their irresponsible behavior, but I could not kill anyone! I wanted to tell God, *This was none of my business. Why me?*

Day after day, the court room filled with the usual spectators. Attention was momentarily drawn away from the trial when an eighteen-year-old drowned in a gravel pit southwest of town. Only fifteen feet from the shore, his companions could not rescue him. The agony of running out of air, on the verge of losing consciousness, and with his last spasmodic breath, he too may have asked, *Why me?*

During the final argument, I stood beside the Assistant Attorney General as he read from his handwritten notes, "Looking at the entire case and all the circumstances, it is clear that Howard and Linda Black did in fact kill Emilie Fischer and Terry Wilson shortly after 1:00 in the morning of October 23, 1976. They planned it, they prepared for it, and they had no better time than the opportunity they had that evening …."

I walked back to his seat with him and sat on the floor next to his chair, knees up, my face on my forearms thinking *it's finally over*. My parents can go back to the farm; David can return to school; the newspapers can focus on something else. Joseph and Jacob Turner, the farmers; Mrs. Wilson, Terry's wife; and all the experts can go home and hopefully have peaceful lives. However, my thoughts were interrupted and then confused by the defense lawyer's beginning statement.

"Do you know my wife and I have a favorite song at the church we attend, and it is entitled, *Let There Be Peace in the World and Let it Begin With Me*…."

*Sir, it's "Let There Be Peace on Earth,"* I corrected him. But maybe he knew a different song than I did. His overly friendly attitude towards the jury distressed me and I buried my face deeper in my arms. But when he used the name, Emilie Fischer, I became attentive, walked up to him, jaw thrust, fists clenched.

"Emilie Fischer is pretty much an innocent bystander in this heartrending tragedy. You don't have anyone who wanted to get even with her," he stated and then paused, surveyed the jury, and nodded his head slowly. I should have felt good about this statement, validated, separated from this entire chaos, but you see it wasn't about me anymore. It was about those who were left to live with what had happened.

Reluctantly, I peered at his notes as he continued his rhetoric— tearing apart all evidence bit by bit using words like *incredulous, idiotic*—until the best witnesses seemed like imbeciles. Even Joseph and his brother, Jacob, were made to feel like probable suspects, simply because they discovered the bodies. My heart ached. Although I believed the Blacks were guilty, my memory of the night's events was vague. I was too drunk, too tired, too hurt. Was there another in the backseat beside the Blacks? Was there another car that met us on that county road, stopped us, pulled Terry out and then me? If so, why didn't Howard and Linda Black tell of it? Was Star, the cussing truck driver, angry enough to kill?

DNA testing was not used until 1986. No attempt was made to make tire impressions on the road of the crime. The undercarriages of cars were not checked for blood samples. There were numerous ballistic tests on a gun or two proving nothing. There were unknown shots taken at Terry's car several days before the homicide. There were murmurs about somebody named Lester with a mysterious connection to Terry who was never asked to testify. With Terry Wilson's past of corrupt and unscrupulous behavior, it's possible that someone else was involved. But who? And what else needed to be uncovered?

Frustrated, I decided to follow the Turner brothers that day. They drove silently, neither speaking, to Jacob's house where Evelyn and Irene waited. In the farmhouse, a pot of coffee and a plate of cookies were already on the table. The men came in the back door. Hugs and a few questions were exchanged. Back at the table, heads bowed in prayer and silence filled the room. A minute later, Joseph said the *Amen*, and Evelyn placed the family Bible in Jacob's hands. He turned to Psalm 119 and read. *Blessed are the undefiled in the way, who walk in the way of the LORD. Blessed are they that keep His testimonies and seek Him with their whole heart. They also do no iniquity; they walk in His ways…. Forever, O LORD, Thy word is settled in heaven…*

The following day, a fire raged through the Farmers Elevator. No one was hurt, and it took some of the attention off the trial. Flames leaped more than fifty feet high and it was a mystery as to how it all began. Fire fighters from surrounding towns came to help. On another news page, a large photo entitled, **Summer Silhouette—A Young Man at Water's Edge**, reminded me of the good times I had had at Big Stone Lake during the summer months. A bit of wistful whimsy occupied my space and for a few moments, I felt young and new.

---

# 9

When the judge instructed the jury to begin their deliberation, I returned to my cozy place under the giant pine on the courthouse lawn to deliberate myself. I studied the clouds, enjoyed the birds and butterflies, and gathered serenity while seven men and five women were locked in a long room with no windows. Twelve persons—each differently designed, each with hurts and concerns of their own, each with their own personal hidden history—given the task to make life-altering decisions for Howard and Linda Black. A restroom was available and coffee provided. As the appointed lunch hour arrived, the judge instructed a bailiff to knock on the jury room door and direct the jurors to prepare for a noon meal recess. Everyone would then be escorted to a small cafe two blocks away for lunch in a private room.

After the meal, the jurors were escorted back to the courthouse and the jury room. During recess and lunch, they were cautioned by the court to avoid discussion of the trial and to ignore media reports of the trial. The jurors could not take notes nor were they allowed daily transcripts to review any testimony. The judge asked them to use their best recollection of the testimony and exhibits. Over a period of days, they moved to 7-5 for acquittal, then 8-4 for acquittal, and then 10-2—a hung jury, a mistrial. They were unable to reach a guilty verdict beyond a reasonable doubt. *You can't get away with murder?* Well, someone did.

Anger, frustration, and sadness washed through me. Quickly. Soon to be replaced by a measure of peace, contentment, and the thought that all of this was in Someone else's hands.

It took nine months for Emilie Fischer to grow in an unknown mother's womb giving her supposedly everything she needed for life in an outside world but with a genetic makeup she would never understand. It took close to nine months from the beginning of my demise to the jury's decision.

The once-packed, paneled, yellow-carpeted, fluorescent-lighted courtroom was silent and mostly empty on that day. Did everyone think it was a given? The verdict: guilty? Howard and Linda Black and their parents were there. A certain rural farm family, my precious parents, who once thought all their dreams had come true with the adoption of a baby girl in November of 1957 were there, aged beyond their years, worn and weary.

Meanwhile, Joseph Turner's personal life had been turned upside down. Remembering the grisly scene, he rarely slept well. He often asked himself, *Who are you, Joseph Turner?* He believed that living out the Christian life was a matter of making a series of right decisions. Somehow, he had failed. Nothing seemed right. During one of his many restless nights, Irene asked him, "Joseph, what is it? Talk to me."

"I don't understand," he mumbled. "How can such a tragedy remain with no resolution? No closure? Imagine Emilie's family, what they must feel."

"I have," Irene said. "Believe me, I have." She rubbed his tension-ridden shoulders and hummed. "This has been a time of trial. We've had it before in our family. And, if you remember Joseph, we got through it one moment at a time. God walked us through every step and every decision we made. It's easy looking back and understanding how He took care of things, but oh so hard not knowing how this will all work out. No matter what happens, Joseph, we have to put it in God's hands."

Guilty or not, the Blacks' lives and that of their extended family were forever changed. They moved to another state no longer feeling accepted in their hometown due to threats and harassment.

The lawyer for the defense stated persuasively, "There will be peace in this community soon." Peace may come, I thought, but it will not be soon. When an issue is unresolved, it is hard to move ahead. It will be months or years before neighbors stop locking their doors again, before they stop looking to see who is creeping down their county road in the middle of the night, before they stop questioning those neighbors who are more suspect than others for whatever reasons seems reasonable to them.

In spite of the murder investigation being reopened immediately after the trial ended and with agents pursuing leads, taking note, checking and re-checking, time passed. People started to look to the things that didn't hurt them—their jobs, the menial routine of life. They celebrated birthdays, took vacations, and planned their Independence Day parties. The Class of '52 gathered for a class reunion. And, tragedy unfortunately struck on Main Street when a forty- two year old father, William Grant, an employee of the Department of Transportation, was crushed by a machine used to roll asphalt and gravel. *For my thoughts are not your thoughts, neither are your ways my ways, saith the LORD.*

David became an American Airlines pilot and was on the aircraft that crashed in May, 1979, Flight 191, just moments after takeoff. Within ninety seconds, the left engine fell off, the plane rolled in midair before plunging to the ground and bursting into flames. All 258 passengers and thirteen crew on board were killed. Eerie quiet, unfamiliar odors, and the sound of sirens soon followed. Haunting. Intent on a career, David never married. Who can understand?

I return to the county road where it all took place, the double homicide, now referred to as a cold case. The rain, the sun, the heavy farm machinery, and daily traffic have erased all signs of a tragedy. However, there is a walk-in-vault in the clerk of court's office with evidence: laboratory reports, autopsy photos, maps, ammunition, shell casings, and a wood remnant found in my hair presumably from the pistol grip, all stored in secured drawers. A dozen bound, hand-written volumes contain the official court reporters' transcripts. One thing however is missing: the gun used to commit the crime, a gun probably with a wooden grip, part of it missing.

Corporate farming became a familiar phrase in the Midwest. Traditional family farms with cows crazing in the fields, chickens scattered about the farmyard, piglets squealing from the pig house, and row upon row of corn and beans to be harvested by one farmer and perhaps his brother became a thing of the past. A combine with as much technological capability as some of the first manned flights to the moon will cut, feed, thresh, separate, clean, and transfer the corn to a large semi tank in minutes... and possibly turn up a rusted pistol with a wood sliver missing from the grip. Will they know what to do with it? Time will tell.

I return to the little country cemetery filled with etched-in crosses and concrete praying hands. My fine feathered friend with his bright red plumage beckons, and I'm on a final mission. I walk by David's burial site, my first love, my last love. I kneel before my parents' grave markers and thank them for loving me, wanting to protect me. Next, I focus on my final physical resting place. I finger the flowers surrounding the cross and study the birth date on the headstone. Yes, I was born November 17, 1957, to a mother, my biological *mamma*, who chose to give me to a family who could better care for me. My parents were good people who longed to keep me safe, protected. I wanted to be a nurse; I wanted to make a difference. I would've been a loving partner, a good momma. But, this thing called life took my earthly existence; I was only eighteen.

A gaggle of teeny-boppers emerge from a quick stop shop in my home town. The place has changed a lot over the years like most towns. We used to hang out at the Sweet Shop on hot summer days dressed in halter tops and frayed jean shorts and lick the soft creamy, cold stuff before it dropped on our bare toes. These girls are clad in short-shorts, flip-flops, and t–shirts, mouths full of braces and prattle. Back pockets bulge with cell phones. Their hands are full of donuts and power drinks. What do they know of time? If my life would have been normal, whatever that is, one of them could have been my granddaughter. I watch them squeeze into a pint-sized car and speed from the parking lot with someplace to go. They loop Main Street several times and end up at someone's house. Much like we used to. Some things don't change.

I'm ready for it to be done. *Judge not, lest you be judged. The judge is standing at the door.* My friend, the cardinal, has situated himself on my headstone, pacing back and forth, and displaying impatience.

"You make me laugh," I tell him.

He begins a melody that fills my heart; he soars, and then sails away until there is no trace of stunning redness. How could the sky have swallowed him up so completely? I search the heavens until I am lost in white, wispy strands; then lifted, then transported to a higher place than I have ever been. A place where there is no need to know specific answers, no need to know *why me?* I hear my mother singing from afar but very clearly, *Blessed assurance, Jesus is mine. Oh, what a foretaste of glory divine. Heir of salvation, purchase of God, born in His spirit, washed in His blood. . ."* Washed in His blood? Washed in His blood! My dream: it's beginning to make sense. Jesus shedding his blood for me; His blood spilling on me, for me. I had been running to the cross. Running to the only One who could be my salvation.

I had stayed because I longed for justice. But wishing doesn't change things; forgiveness does. There is a joy in my heart I cannot explain as the sacred curtains of heaven open. ... *and there before me is a white horse, whose rider is called Faithful and True. With justice he judges...* A great number of people, so many I cannot count them, wear white robes and wave palm branches, seeing me not as a victim of cruel circumstances but as God intended me to be. Perfect.

Grandma Hulda, Grandpa Arthur, Michael, Samuel, my parents, David, and Momma .... *Momma.*

"EMILIE?"

I can't take my eyes off her.

"EMILIE!"

"Yes, dear God?"

"YOU HAVE ONE MORE THING TO DO."

"Yes...."

"SURRENDER..." God tells me.

"But I need to share the good news about your Kingdom...."

"YOU JUST DID IT."

"What do you mean?"

"YOUR STORY. YOU TOLD IT AS ONLY YOU CAN TELL IT."

---

# 10

Years pass. *With the LORD, a day is like a thousand years and a thousand years is like a day.* Joseph's wife, Irene, dies of cancer. He keeps busy visiting his daughters, and when they're not together, writing letters to each other, continuing a tradition Irene started when each daughter left home to begin her own life. Keeping up with the grandkids' birthdays, serving on a church committee or two, and farming fill his days. With Irene gone, the house feels empty and cold. As the tape on the carefully written Bible verses ages and loses its grip, the verses slip to the floor. Joseph patiently reapplies a fresh strip of tape and maintains his memory work. The verses and Irene's handwriting help him miss her less, if that is possible.

Discovering two dead bodies along a county road is forever etched in his memory. The way the trial was mishandled and the fact that it is a cold case is a thorn in his side. Joseph, the task-master, the man who got things done, came to realize there were some things out of his control. He often thought, *What could I have done differently?* He believed he was a servant in God's kingdom and should know and pass on the message of truth in all things. He often thought of 1 Thessalonians 5:23, *May God Himself, the God of peace, sanctify me through and through. May my whole spirit, soul, and body be kept blameless at the coming of our Lord Jesus Christ.* And he prayed, *If there is a way, dear LORD, to resolve all this, reveal it to me.... Thy kingdom come, Thy will be done.*

One morning, feeling a little out of the ordinary, he skipped breakfast and left the house to do his usual chores. A few cats followed at his heels as he carried a bucket of cracked corn to the pig house and fed a mother sow snuggled with her new piglets. To make sure all was in order, he checked the toolshed; the massive barn, where a few swallows chirped; and then the machine shed.

Walking back towards the house, he noted the cardinal perched on his mailbox. "Waiting for something?" Joseph asked the bird and rubbed his jaw. The bird puzzled him, showing up at unpredictable times. Joseph, short of breath and thinking he needed to eat, headed to the back door where he took off his chore clothes and boots. In the kitchen he sat at the table to rest.

A daughter, who lived nearby, stopped by later in the morning to find Joseph on the kitchen floor, dead. A heart attack had ended his life.

Each daughter kept a keepsake or two—a piece of furniture, a favorite pie dish. Going through the roll top desk in the dining room, they found a large manila envelope filled with a packet of yellowing news articles, dated 1977. Yes, *the trial*, they recalled. It was all there: the witness statements, the deliberations, and the reminder that it was still a cold case—a major event in their dad's life without closure.

"He can let it go now," one of them said.

"We should probably get these news articles to Jacob," another said. "He'll know what to do with them."

"Jacob will miss him as much as we do," someone murmured. "They went through so much together—the farming, those Bethel Bible classes they attended together. They used to quiz each other on Bible verses!"

"Good heavens," another chimed in. "I thought that was just a mom and dad thing."

"Have you been in Jacob and Evelyn's house recently?" one of them asked.

⋅⋅◆◆◆⋅⋅

For everyone, aging is inevitable. Joseph's brother, Jacob, worked harder to get simple things done. When he looked in the mirror, he didn't recognize the man he saw. Short in stature, slumping shoulders, sagging skin. Somedays when he put coveralls and overshoes on mid-morning to do the few remaining chores, he was reminded by Evelyn that he had already completed them. Mentally and physically, he was fading away.

Jacob, now in his eighties, no longer looked forward to planting in the spring or harvesting in the fall. His farm buildings were silent except for a few chickens in the barn and the occasional possum and other rodents seeking an easy shelter. He was tired …..

Nursing a lukewarm cup of coffee one Saturday morning, Jacob heard a tapping at the back door. He looked out the window to see his son's car. John Turner was in his thirties, a graduate from the state university with a degree in Ag Science. A cardinal chirped from the hood of John's car. Jacob didn't know whether to curse the bird or bless him. The feathered friend seemed to have made himself at home on the Turner farms.

"Been a while, Son," Jacob said welcoming him with a shoulder hug. Without asking, he set a cup of coffee on the table for his son and re-filled his own. Evelyn's home-made lemon bars, John's favorite, were already beckoning on the table. Jacob wondered about that; Evelyn hadn't been up to doing much lately.

"Your mom's still in bed," Jacob said. "Can't seem to get enough rest lately. The arthritis; it wears her out."

"I should have called first," John said. "But I was driving by, saw you were at home, and thought I'd drop in."

"Good to see you," Jacob answered but knew that there was more than *just dropping in* by the look on John's face. "What is it John?" he asked. "Hope nothing is wrong. Your family all right?"

"Sure, Missy and the kids, all good," John answered, took a sip, and looked around at the scraps of paper with Bible verses scattered about the room. "You and Mom, you took all those Bible classes and memorized all those verses. Uncle Joseph and Aunt Irene did the same, didn't they?"

"Yeah, we actually enjoyed it. We quizzed each other, talked about what each one meant to us, for us. We had a good life, here." He paused, in deep thought. "I miss Joseph. We did everything together. Time passes; the farm isn't the same."

"I guess that's what I want to talk to you about. This place, here." John took off his John Deere cap and hooked it to the back of his chair. "I got an idea I want to run by you."

Within minutes, John Turner shared his interest in buying the farm, filling the hog lot again, getting chicklets in the spring, and planting the usual corn and soybeans. Jacob listened intently, nodding off and on. Evelyn shuffled out in her faded robe, warm socks and slippers on her feet.

"Sit down, Mom." John said. "I'll get you your coffee."

John gave his dad time to think, set the coffee in front of his Mom, gave her a pat on the shoulder and winked at her. She nodded her head perceptively. Jacob looked at his wife. Always so tired, he thought. The housework, the garden—he understood it was a load she shouldn't have to bear any longer.

John interrupted his thoughts. "You know Missy's been after me for years to get the kids on a farm. She has this big idea of growing vegetables and strawberries for farmers' markets. Wants to give the kids a 4-H project, that kind of thing...."

"Kids need to be kept busy," Jacob finally stated. "You have a good family, good kids, John; it's not easy in today's world to do that." It was John's turn to be quiet. He knew his request to buy the family farm was asking a lot—a big financial undertaking for his family and a life change for his parents. Jacob got up from the table to get a drink of water and looked out the kitchen window over the sink; Evelyn went to stand beside him; words were exchanged as she rubbed his aging shoulder muscles. A minute later, Jacob returned to the table with a smile animating his weather-worn, aging face. He was seeing himself a part of a bigger picture.

"What is it?" John asked, perplexed.

"I'm just imagining the grandkids running around this farm. Bringing it alive again. It's a great idea that Missy has to keep the kids busy with 4-H projects." They shook hands as John left and agreed to work out the many details later. Outside, the cardinal strutted in front of the house.

"Got a new friend?" John asked his dad indicating the bird.

"More like an old friend," Jacob answered and laughed. "Can't seem to get rid of the silly thing. It's determined about something. Just can't figure out what it is. Gonna be as old as I am before he's a gonner."

<hr />

KATHLEEN STAUFFER

# EPILOGUE

*Jesus also said, "The Kingdom of God is like a farmer who scatters seed on the ground. Night and day, while he's asleep or awake, the seed sprouts and grows, but he does not understand how it happens. The earth produces the crops on its own. First a leaf blade pushes through, then the heads of wheat are formed, and finally the grain ripens."*

John Turner started each day with devotions, his wife at the kitchen table beside him. Today's verse from Mark 4 prompted discussion.

"He's at work in us even when we don't see the results," Missy said. "That's really a comfort, isn't it?"

"I think of the legacy my parents left us," John answered. "This house, the farm, and more significantly, their faith in God."

"Oh my goodness, those Bible verses," Missy giggled. "I find them every once in a while, stashed in a drawer or cupboard; I get them out and read them. Sometimes, it's just what I need."

John nodded his head in agreement, checked his watch, and looked outside. There were chores to do. The goats, newly acquired chicks, and a couple of calves needed their morning rations. He placed his unfinished coffee in the sink.

"Like I said, God is at work even when we're not seeing the results, John. Your dad knew that. Both Turner brothers were task-masters. They were also gentle, Godly men." Missy smiled, happy herself, to have such a Godly man as her husband and the father of their children.

John kissed his wife on the lips and left the house that day to be his own kind of task master. By this time, his footprints were all over the farm, in and out of the various buildings. A hog shed was now used for starting seedlings. Part of the barn was a storage area for carts and crates used when they took their produce to the farmers' markets in nearby towns. Life had been good for them.

After feeding the animals, he headed to his old pickup with a box of remaining bare roots. It was a school day. The kids and Missy had worked Saturday in the garden produce plot. Wanting to get a good look at the kids' 4-H project, John had promised that he would finish the job for them. It was early spring and a bit nippy, but the air smelled fresh, clean, and filled with possibilities. He drove the short distance into the field and hopped out. The kids and Missy had done a good job. He noticed the carefully measured out rows, twelve inches apart, with plants about every twenty inches. He placed the box of strawberry roots on the ground and knelt down. The cardinal marched beside him.

"Don't you have anything better to do?" John joked. The bird had become a family pet, predictably present at chore time. When the children were outdoors playing, it followed them around at their heels like a lost chick or watched with interest from a bough above. The kids had even given him a name—Michael.

"Why *Michael*?" he had asked Bennet, his oldest son. Bennet, at ten years of age, often showed wisdom beyond his years. However, at this question, he eyed his dad speculatively, shrugged his shoulders, and returned to the tree house he was building.

Loosening the soil with a small shovel, John held a strawberry plant by its crown, gently spread the roots open, placed it in the soil, and then covered it with dirt. Sliding the box with him, he crept forward on his knees, inserting a plant every twenty inches until he came to the end of the row. One bare root remained in the box.

Standing, he surveyed the plot and realized that an empty spot remained in one of the rows. An open space, where Michael paced. The bird whistled a piercing *come hither, come hither*. John stepped carefully between the plants to that spot. As he knelt down he felt something sharp. With his small shovel, he prodded the black earth, and struck something hard, metallic. Brushing away the dirt with his glove, he pulled a pitted and scratched gun from the earth. A gun with a wooden grip, a sliver of it missing.

# Jacqueline's Story: Do Not Fear

The horizon is raw-red; I turn and look west. A desolate highway and the tail lights of Tammy's car make me wonder how she came up with this god-forsaken town. Was I a fool to count on her to find me a place to live? A glance at my little daughter steels my resolve. Any place is better than watching Clarissa die by slow degrees. If it had been only myself who was suffering, I would have stayed with Claude for the sake of the children. But when Clarissa stopped talking and then stopped eating, I knew that her father was destroying her soul as well as mine.

I pick up my oldest child with one arm, my suitcase with the other, push open the door with 115 Main Street carved on it, and climb twenty-six steps. Jazz music and the smell of frying bacon drift from the apartment on the left. My stomach lurches.

Using the key from Tammy, I turn to the unit on the right and push it in the keyhole. The door swings open. I step in, release my still-sleepy child to the floor, and sit on the suitcase. A bed with springs and rag-tag mattress, a small refrigerator with a monotonous hum, and yellowed shades hanging at various levels in the windows stare back at me. My box of meager household items hits the floor beside me and disrupts my dazed spell. Someone squeezes my shoulder, and I wipe tears away with the back of my hand. A man dressed in a bath robe open to his navel and smelling of bacon and cologne stands above me.

"Want to eat?" He asks.

I pick up my daughter and follow him to his apartment across the hall. Clarissa and I eat the greasy bacon and wipe our plates clean with toast as he studies me. He covers my hand with his; I ball my fist; he squeezes tighter and turns my fist. Looking at my scarred wrist, he nods his head knowingly. I feel awkward, powerless, and desperately miss the child I left behind.

He follows me back to my room and brings a black and white television set. "Was here before," he explains. "We'll get you a couch," he says.

"Do you know Tammy, my sister-in-law?" I speak for the first time.

"Only the name," he states. "Don' need to know nothin' else. Better that way." He acts as if we are sharing secrets.

"Do you have an extra blanket?" Clarissa shivers beside me; the wind rattles our windows. He leaves and comes back with a blanket, sheets, and pillows—dingy and smelling like him—and I am reminded of not so long ago: hanging laundry on the line in a summer sun with two little girls playing hide-and-go-seek under sheets flapping in the wind.

Night comes. I do not sleep. Cold rain beats down on the roof. So much to think about: Cassandra, the daughter left behind, what must she be thinking? Will Claude try to find us? Tomorrow, I must look for work and make a plan to get Cassandra. I pick my brain for something to hang on to. *Fear not for I am with thee* comes to mind. I know that "I" is God. Why does he feel so far away? How could he possibly have allowed this to happen?

• • ✦ ✦ ✦ • •

I smooth Clarissa's hair away from her forehead and remember being a little girl. I never missed Sunday School. The booklets had pictures of smiling parents walking hand-in-hand with their children into a church. I wanted to take a crayon and black out the parents' faces, but I was an obedient child. How do you tell anyone that your parents are abnormal? They didn't act like other parents. My mother had a heart of stone, and my father's behavior was not unusual for a man thus chained to a cold, cold woman. I wanted to run away and be free, but how could I be free with an ax buried in my heart? As a child, I could not put my finger on the reasons. I could not fix anything.

I remember being Clarissa's age and climbing an apple tree on a fall day. My bare foot slipped, and I plummeted to the damp earth below, stunned. Mother's face hovered above me, and I heard her say, "Ralph?"— my father's name. She didn't drop to her knees, she didn't say *my* name, she didn't scream. In the emergency room, a doctor shined a flashlight in my eyes. "How ya doin' little one?" I had to stop myself from reaching out my arms and begging, "Take me, please." I walked out of the examination room with a nurse holding my hand to see my mother sitting with arms crossed wearing her mad face. Dad was looking at his watch; his left leg was twitching. The nurse gave my backside a slight shove in their direction. No hugs, no kisses, no—*So glad you're okay, Jacqueline.* I stared out the window of the backseat on the way home, my forehead pressed on the cold window.

School was a relief of sorts. I was independent and curious and learned ahead of others. I had nice clothes and was fed well but I felt that my classmates were suspicious of me—like they knew something about me or my family that was not good. I pretended to have an invisible shield that protected me from others' stares and occasional sarcasm. During rest time, I closed my eyes and imagined a new family.

My teacher reprimanded me for daydreaming and doodling on my papers. I already knew the spelling words. I didn't need to memorize the math facts. All this stuff was already in my head, somehow. Some of the tests, however, tried to trick me. If you ask a question like, "Which word does not fit: add, subtract, multiply, increase?" Of course, the answer is add. All the rest have eight letters, right? When I pointed this out, the teachers referred to me as overly-sensitive and used the word petulant, as in, *most of your other answers are right, why do you care about this one?*

In high school, classmates called me snobbish, hard to get to know. So, I ran with the bad girls. You know, the ones who smoke and drink. The bad girls said I was soft, a goodie-two-shoes. I didn't smoke, drink, or swear, but they accepted me—a strange bird.

I don't know what caused my parents to be the way they were. However, I felt that things were never right around our house. Mother was detached; Father drank. Mother never glimpsed my father's soul or mine or considered our needs. Pain was routinely swept under the rug. I could say my mother fought depression or I could say she thrived on being melancholy. My dad escaped into another woman's arms. Maybe that is why he saw no need for either of us.

I became as wild as someone like me could become. I stayed out late, didn't come home at times, treated my parents with scorn. I felt trapped in a miserable life. There were times, during periods of deep solitude, that I felt a sense of mystery. A sense that someone was looking for me. To rescue me. Was this the God of my Sunday School? I searched for him one night when the sensation was especially strong, running blindly through the dark, stumbling, crying, and laughing, not knowing why and wondering if I was the crazy one. I ended up on Grand Avenue in front of my father's business. He sold appliances—refrigerators, stoves, washing machines. Cynthia lived in the apartment above the store. She was Dad's right-hand-gal, as Dad called her, answering the phone, doing the bookwork. That was the night I saw them. He was kissing her, embracing her in front of her apartment window for all the world to see. My feet were cemented to the sidewalk. I felt like I was living at the edge of an abyss, waiting for someone to push me over the rim.

After that, when Dad talked about Cynthia doing something at the appliance store, I would interrupt, and say, "Do you mean, Cyn?" He would clear his throat before continuing; my mother would leave the room.

I read somewhere that attachments make us human and decided that even though my dad was sinning with Cynthia, she at least made it possible for him to survive my mother's passionless soul. So, when Claude Jesse Walwyn came into my life, I decided to be *human* and simply jumped the abyss—from one edge to the other.

I met Claude at a late-night bash at an abandoned farmhouse. Groups of kids hung out drinking, chattering—each one trying to impress someone, anyone. Claude was by himself, in a corner, scanning the crowd, a bottle of beer in his hand. I caught him staring at me. I watched him saunter towards me: he was tall, lanky, and vaguely alarming.

"Hey," he said. His voice was husky, deep.

"Hi," I murmured, feeling naïve and small.

"Never seen you before." He emphasized *you*, like I was something special, something desired.

"First time," I replied.

"First time?" He chuckled, a sound coming from his belly. His hand tugged my pony tail and stayed there.

"Stop it," I muttered. I felt silly and in over my head.

"You don't mean that." His breath was warm and moist in my ear. He turned and walked away. Like a moth drawn to a burning bulb, I followed.

We were soon in his car, his right hand half way up my thigh, his left hand turning the radio on. We sat that way for maybe a half hour or so and then he motioned for me to leave. As I started to close the passenger door, he told me that he would see me the next night.

That's how it all started. It became an every night thing. His strong arms, his leanness, his hands all over me—I couldn't resist him; I was physically starved. He never told me he loved me. He never told me I was beautiful. However, I chose to think he loved me without ever knowing the meaning of love and was soon carrying his child.

Looking back, I realize that Claude's confident, possessive persona was a sham, and the mysterious air he assumed was a cover for his own insecurities.

In spite of the fact that Claude said he didn't want anyone around on our wedding day; Deirdre, Claude's mother, was there along with his brother, Douglas, and his wife, Tammy. My parents called Claude Walwyn white-trash and disowned me. We moved into Claude's childhood home, outside the small town of Greenville, where I soon realized that the name Walwyn carried a curse of its own.

Nevertheless, I nested. I felt like the first person on earth to ever carry and bear a child, and I told myself that I would be a better parent than either of mine. I would be warm, loving, and protective. I even had aspirations of turning this whole shame thing of being a "Walwyn" around. But after Clarissa's birth, depression set in along with the everyday reality of living with a man like Claude—a man with secrets, a man with demons of his own. He spent long hours in the cellar under our house muttering—something about *what kills the skunk is the publicity it gives itself*—and working with hammer and nails. He would ignore me and Clarissa for days. He expected us to live on next to nothing. After realizing Claude was not really into me or our child and that I was destined to live a life of poverty as a Walwyn, I took a knife from the kitchen drawer one night and walked out on the porch. I considered the stars and felt I could not survive. With no more thought, I sliced the knife across my wrist. After the initial shooting agnony, the world became muffled until I heard Clarissa from afar crying, "Mama! Mama!"—perhaps some nightmare of her own had awakened her. The reality that I had almost abandoned her terrified me. Wiping the blood and tears on my apron, I rushed to her crib. Picking her up and feeling her warmth, I felt her innocence. I could never leave her.

⋅⟡⟡⟡⋅

The years passed. Routine became my friend: the laundry, the meager meals, discovering the birds and bugs in the nearby grove with Clarissa, an occasional conversation with Deirdre who lived across the road. And, then, Cassandra arrived. Clarissa delighted in her sister, and I delighted in them both. Due to my attempts to do everything I could to protect my little ones, I awkwardly approached the pastor of the country church near our house. Although I had not been attending the services, he agreed to baptize Cassandra and Clarissa in a private service.

I invited Deirdre, their grandmother. She came dressed in her usual attire—black sweats and combat boots. I was relieved it was a private service. Claude used the comment *what hurts the skunk is the publicity it gives itself* and refused to come. With his arms folded over his chest, he watched the four of us walk to the church that day. During supper, he declared that the girls and I were never to speak to Deirdre, again. She was a strange lady, often sour, so I didn't argue his decision. He also commanded that we were to stay away from the church.

I began to wonder what he was afraid of.

There were moments of delight—goofiness, dancing, singing—especially when Claude's brother, Douglas, and his wife, Tammy, showed up for the holidays. During these times, Tammy became my confidant. She seemed to understand my issues although she said little about her own. Good food—in spite of our minimal circumstances— fun conversations and games gave us a reason to go on. That is, until that final Thanksgiving we were all together, when Douglas showed his blackest side. I wanted to give Clarissa and Cassandra happiness, security, but the wolf and more was at the door and on that particular night was in our very house. I no longer saw Douglas as fun-loving. There are no words for his kind of immoral conduct; Claude's excuses for him were unforgiveable. I wanted to be angry with Tammy; I would miss her.

Claude continued to degenerate. He tinkered with his rusty junk throughout the day while I tried to scrape together three meals. He drank away every penny in a house that was falling apart. I came to understand that Claude was an alcoholic, an irresponsible drunk. He was also an extreme introvert and a miser. He was uncomfortable with his own family, and he seemed to resent the fact that we needed money to live. Money which he would prefer to spend on his precious booze.

After that Thanksgiving holiday with his brother, Douglas, and my sister-in-law when everything and I mean everything went awry, I knew I would leave. However, I had no idea how. In spite of Claude's warning to stay away from the church, I approached it one afternoon after hearing music. The lady organist? She would have listened; I just didn't know what to say. I lingered at the school. Again, I didn't know what to say. I had dreamed of taking the stigma away from the Walwyn name. What I had to say would make it worse. Although Deirdre lived across the road, Claude had prevented any contact with her, and with her nick-name, *the witch*, a name the townspeople had dropped on her, what help could I possibly expect.

After weeks of sleepless nights and private phone conversations with Tammy, I made a plan to escape. Tammy was to pick me up at midnight—a time Claude was usually in a drunken sleep. She had rented a place for me for the first month. I would get a job, start to earn an income and then return to get the girls. However, in the middle of that night, in the middle of a hot argument with Claude as I was ready to leave in the car with Tammy, Clarissa runs from the house—her white nightgown whipping against her legs, saying "Mamma!" What else could I do? I scooped her up, threw us both into the car, and we were off. Gunshots pierced the night. My heart stopped.

"We must go back!" I screamed.

"There's no going back," Tammy replied.

--- ◆◆◆◆◆ ---

*There's no going back, there's no going back,* like a broken record plays in my head; I try to sleep.

"Breakfast on the table," he says. It's the guy across the hall, the man who Tammy found, the man whose apartment I am subletting. I pull Clarissa from the bed and follow him. Starving, as we had not eaten since breakfast yesterday, I stay dressed in the only nightgown I have packed and Clarissa in hers. He takes my hand. I don't pull away.

"Who are you? Why are you doing this?" I ask.

"You need help. I can give it."

"Your name?"

"Henry," he says proudly, "Henry Cane." I note his own scar, zig-zag bumps of flesh, running from his left ear down to his Adam's apple. His hair is slicked back with oil; his fingernails are long. I don't like what I see; I don't like how I feel. I need food. I need a job. I need to enroll my child in school. I need transportation to rescue my other child. Henry's needs are different than mine. A strange man, dressed only in a robe, who invites you to breakfast, has needs. And, I ask myself, *Did Tammy, my sister-in-law, someone I trusted, realize that this would become my life?*

I find a job cleaning rooms at the Motel 6. The money I try to save, Henry takes from me. We eat from his table and he pays the rent, he explains. I condemn myself each night, call myself a failure, and fear for Cassandra. Is Claude punishing her because of my disappearance? Is she eating, sleeping, going to school?

A school bus picks up Clarissa; she doesn't complain. I feel I am losing her, too, even though she lives with me. She feels so far away. It is as if she knows I cannot be trusted to take care of her. I often find her at the window staring off into space—latching on to nothing I can see. Weeks pass, months, and then a year or more. I think of my left-behind daughter with every sigh, and lose track of time. Then, a letter comes and time stands still. My sister-in-law, Tammy, writes and states her concerns about Cassandra's welfare and why haven't I returned to get her? At supper, I beg Henry to take me back to Greenville to get Cassandra. He takes my hand, turns it over, and rubs the scar on my wrist until it hurts.

"Stop," I say.

"Stop," he mimics. "Stop what? Stop feeding you and your whiny brat? Stop paying your rent? Just what would you like me to stop, Jaqueline?" He kisses the mutilated welt—and I am reminded of a time and place and the blood and tears when I could not take my life because I could not leave my child.

I take the plates and silverware to the sink. Clarissa whimpers beside me. I hand her a towel and say, "Dry the dishes." He watches us, his hands folded over his rounded belly. I place the dishes in the cupboard and take my child's hand. We descend the twenty-six steps down to Main Street where one street light casts a dim glow. We walk around the block with Clarissa clinging to my side. Barking dogs, a few houses with televisions throwing trivial sounds out into the night, crickets—but there is no one to help.

Back in our room, I cannot sleep. I am thankful that Clarissa breathes gently beside me. I hear his footsteps. I smell his smell. He pulls me across the hall to his apartment. I know the routine. My face is covered with tears of hatred and shame. He rolls over and sleeps. I take the steps back across the hall, slip in to bed, and pull my oldest daughter close. Again, thinking of the one I left behind. I am broken, weary, and no longer worthy to be called "mother."

Morning comes. Clarissa boards the bus. I walk towards a steeple pointing to the sky and enter a church. There is a banner bathed in early morning sunlight. ...*I am convinced that neither death nor life, neither angels nor demons, neither the present nor the future, nor any powers, neither height or depth, nor anything else in all creation will be able to separate us from the love of God that is in Christ Jesus our Lord.* And, I remember the childhood verse I memorized: *Fear not for I am with thee.*

I stay in this place where I feel love until I must go. It's a better, more hopeful day.

At supper, again, I bring it up.

"She needs me, Henry; she is my child; I must get her," I beg.

"You can't possibly take care of her. You can't take care of the child you have. Plus, you owe me, Jacqueline." He says this calmly as if talking to a child. I cannot look at him. He disgusts me: his oiled hair, his hairy chest, the way he picks at his teeth after eating.

A large lump forms in my throat. How could I possibly have thought that he would be, could be this generous? I owed him? He already took every penny of my pay check.

"What do I need to do?" I ask. Henry ignores me, goes into his bedroom, and closes the door.

A week and more passes. Something is wrong with Clarissa. The school has sent social workers with questions I cannot answer. I receive a raise at work and tuck the few extra dollars away and dream of going back to Greenville to rescue my youngest daughter. However, reality always follows the daydream— can I give Cassandra a better life than what she is living? I curse myself for leaving and secretly hope that Claude is looking for us, and I write a letter. Not to Claude, but I write to Deirdre, his mother, my children's grandmother—the sour, old lady, the one they called *the witch*, who lived across the road from us. Someone needs to know; someone needs to understand.

On a Saturday night, Clarissa and I watch the black and white TV that Henry has provided. Her forehead is warm; I know she is sick, but I can do nothing about it. He walks in with several empty boxes, turns the television off, and says to pack up. Shocked, I feel the contents of the room whirl around me.

"Why?" I ask.

Henry opens the cupboards and chucks our meager possessions in the boxes.

"Where are we going?" I ask.

"Tomorrow morning. Be ready." He states as he leaves.

Clarissa pulls on my arm and says, "Mom?" I pull her close, run my fingers through her tangled hair, as a woozy feeling overwhelms me. Is it possible that we are returning to Greenville to rescue Cassandra?

The sky is an icy blue when I hear Henry tramping up and down the steps. Soon, the three of us are in a car. Clarissa shivers under her thin coat and coughs. Henry fiddles with a radio station. The static feels like pin pricks as we speed off towards an unknown horizon. Hours pass, and the realization that we are not headed to Greenville fills me with rage. I consider jumping from the car with Clarissa in my arms. I consider killing Henry, taking his car, and driving to Greenville, myself. I look at the back of his neck, I look on the floor for something to strike him with, and, then, I feel foolish.

We stop at a gas station. I get the key for the restroom while Henry fills the tank. The floor is damp. It smells like urine. Clarissa looks sickly. I pull her from the restroom and return the key. In the station, there are people. I look into their faces, try to make eye contact. Is there anyone who can help us? A woman whisks her own small child away from us as if we are contagious.

I cannot tell you about the next months and years of my life. Much I do not remember; much I choose not to remember; the rest would do you no good to know. Suffice it to say, that my previous isolated life in

Greenville seems like heaven. Henry moves us to another small town, to another dingy apartment. I am introduced to a world that I had been oblivious to. I do not ask questions; I do not want to know. To say I hate it would be an understatement of huge proportions. Clarissa is often sick and misses school. People come to our house and threaten to take her away. I have to let her go. I failed Cassandra by leaving her; I failed Clarissa by taking her.

I make it my goal to do everything I can to get my children back, but I live in despair. I know it will take a miracle for this to happen. Henry is typically out at night. He often expects me to come with him. I hope something awful happens to him so I can be free.

One morning I find his clothes, reeking of sweat and torn, dropped by our bedside. As he sleeps, I see that his hands, arms, and face are raked with scratches. A large bruise covers one forearm and one of his eyes puffs to twice its size. I don't ask questions. But knowing this gives me permission to steal from him. It would be wrong stealing from a good person, but an evil person? I go through every single cupboard, drawer, pocket to steal a dollar here, a dollar there hoping he will not miss the very little that I take. I grow even more fearful—what could he do because I took from him? I take a small carving knife from the back of a kitchen drawer, wrap it in a washrag, and bury it in the bottom of my purse. On some days, I feel empowered because of what I am doing. On other days, I cannot place one foot in front of the other; my emotional burden is too great. I write another letter to Deirdre.

"Get up, get out of bed. You need to work!" Henry hisses.

"I'm sick," I say.

"Doesn't matter. Get dressed. I'll be in the car."

Waves of heat and then cold sweep over me. I shiver, I'm out of breath; I dress. On the way to work, I fall asleep. Henry pushes me from the car. "You'll be okay. Buck up." I no longer think of killing him. I do not have the strength.

With one look at me, my supervisor sticks me in her car and takes me to the hospital. Pneumonia, they say. No insurance, I say. We'll take care of you, they say. And, I sleep. Clarissa is gone; Henry is not with me. Alone with my body at last, I feel my breathing. I give in to the pain—the aches from sickness, the aches of life—and I wonder about the me inside.

Pictures from the past slide in and out of my head—a baby dropped from the second floor, a young girl wandering through brambles and bushes, a cry in the night, gunshots, a car ride to nowhere. Because of the illness, because death knocks at my door, I learn of services that help me to run. I am ready.

A county social worker leads me to her car. I have a worn bag with my identification in it, a bottle of antibiotics, the knife; I have the clothes on my back. These helping people know only a part of my story. Getting away from Henry is easy. Since Claude had made no attempt to find me, I determine that Henry will do the same.

I get another job cleaning motel rooms in another small town. Again, I live above Main Street, and I wonder about the cycle in my life that keeps repeating itself. Main Street, deserted highways, empty life. There are times I do not know what month of the year it is. The seasons slip through my fingers. I cannot grab hold of anything. And, then, there are days and weeks that seem to linger forever.

A letter arrives from Cassandra, a little girl I no longer know—a letter that halts everything. She addresses the envelope with my name, and, then, *address unknown*, and then, *will someone please deliver*. It breaks my heart and, yet, I am hopeful. *Someone* knows where I am! *Deirdre?* I put it in the bottom of my purse with the knife, get it out and place it in my smock pocket at work. I touch it often and memorize her every word.

I learn that my oldest daughter, Clarissa, is adopted into a family. I stop myself from imagining what life could have been. I no longer dream of being a mother to two little girls—with picnics, dances on the front lawn, hide and seek in the grove. It hurts too much. I do remember the banner in the church. I remember the childhood verse—*do not fear, I am with you.* I work. I keep a small apartment neat and clean. I attend a little church with a small congregation. I sit in the back and leave early. The preacher's words about love, forgiveness, by grace are you saved, and a heavenly father fill me. I do not understand much of it, and, yet, I leave somewhat contented.

Walking home from church on Sunday morning, I hear a car behind me. It stops beside me. The smell of men's cologne mixed with grease floats through the open window.

"Jaqueline," a man says. "Get in."

Without thinking, my hand reaches for the handle. I pull it back quickly.

"Jacqueline," Henry repeats. "Get in." He says it softly, in a way that he knows he has me. I stare at him briefly. He has aged. Bags of darkness surround his eyes. One eye droops.

"What happened?" I ask. Did he have a stroke? Has he been ill? I wanted to kill this man, and here he was.

"I'm back. I'm here to help," he answers.

*I'm here to help* takes me back to the first time I met this man, and I know Henry's words are a lie.

Don't need it." I say and continue walking. Henry follows, the hood of the car almost rubbing my thigh.

"You forgot, Jacqueline," he says, this time his voice rising. "You owe me. In fact, you owe me lots, Jacqueline. Get in the car!" he shouts. The streets are empty. It's Sunday morning. People are still at church or in their beds sleeping in. I feel the hardness of the knife in my purse as it beats against my leg with every step. I know it's sharp. I've tested it. I make a 180 degree turn and run several blocks back to the church. As parishioners are leaving, I rush back up the steps and collapse in the back pew of the sanctuary. I rest my head on my forearms and hide my face, gasping for air.

The bench creaks; someone sits beside me. "Let me introduce myself," he says.

"I know who you are," I say, out of breath, sweaty, unworthy to be in his presence. I see the toes of his black shiny shoes and the white folds of a robe covering the laces.

"Well, I don't know your name, but I have noticed you leave early every Sunday," he says. "Can I help you?" His fingertips lightly touch my upper arm.

"I need a ride, a ride home," I explain. He doesn't ask why. I soon hear the jangle of keys and follow him.

"Are you feeling threatened?" he asks. We are parked outside my upstairs apartment, and I wonder what the other church goers will think of a pastor sitting in a car with a woman like me on a Sunday morning.

"Sort of." I admit. I look around.

"Are you going to be okay?" he asks.

I get out of the car and say *thank you* thinking I will never be okay.

I am more observant of my surroundings. I lock the door with a bolt and slide a chair under it each night. I watch cars as they pass. We clean in teams when doing the house-keeping at The Staff Motel so I am never alone at work. The pastor visits me occasionally and I can't help but eventually tell him of Cassandra and Clarissa, my two daughters, no longer mine. He holds my hand in both of his when I greet him after church. I ask for his prayers.

I keep a calendar. Years pass, but I know how old my daughters are. I celebrate their birthdays without them; I sing; I light a single candle. I imagine what they must look like as pre-teens, then teenagers. Do they do well in school? Do they have friends? Do they even think of me? Of course, I am most concerned about Cassandra— the child left-behind.

A letter comes from someone I do not remember, Anne Christiansen. She writes that she is from Greenville, plays the organ at the church where my babies were baptized, the church near the house Claude and I lived in so long ago. Anne offers something I have only been able to dream about. She tells me I can stay at her place while I become reacquainted with my Cassandra. A little girl who did not forget her mother, a little girl who has been longing for me all these years. She is a young woman now. I sob uncontrollably and wonder how this can be possible? I am not worthy to be called mother. I did not protect or provide for either child. I tried, but I failed miserably. How does the One others refer to as "God" consider one like me that my prayers would be answered?

Feeling hopeful, I correspond with Anne over the months. A date is set.

I take a leave from work, pack a few things, and look into the mirror. I do not recognize this Jacqueline. She is worn-out, wrinkled, colorless. Can I do this? *Do not fear* comes to mind, and I know that there are surely others, like the pastor of our church, who sincerely care. Anne Christiansen arrives, and I get into a station wagon with this lady who has written me letters, this lady who has made it possible for me to return to Cassandra.

"How much do I owe you?" I ask. I straighten my coat and look at her sideways. She looks to be in her fifties. Her hair is nicely coifed. She is dressed in a royal blue sweater set. Even her shoes are blue. She studies me momentarily as if to get a connection. Even though I feel shabby sitting next to her in her car, I feel acceptance which I cannot explain.

"You owe me nothing," she says. "Your daughter has been waiting a lifetime for this."

Anxiety washes through me and knocks my breath away. *Waiting a lifetime?*

"She will be disappointed. I cannot do this," I say and stutter in gibberish even I do not understand. Anne takes my hand and holds it as she pulls away from the curb. The drone of the wheels turning on the highway comforts me. I take a deep breath; I'm going home….

"I know Cassandra very well." Anne interrupts my thoughts. "She is a godly young woman. Clarissa, your other daughter?" She waits as if it is a question. "She plans to come as well."

"You know them?" I ask, flabbergasted. I feel nauseous and look over my shoulder indicating to Anne that we need to turn around even though I, too, have been waiting a lifetime for this very thing to happen. "I'm sorry," I say. "I can't do this."

"You can do this, Jacqueline," Anne says. "Lots of prayers have been said for this day and for your family. Surely, this is difficult, but I believe God's hand is involved in all this." She pauses, passes a car, and again picks up my hand. "I could have helped you many years ago." She takes a deep breath. "I just didn't know how. We'll do this together. I'll stay with you." I press my hand to my hammering heart and think, *Fear not, fear not.*

We arrive in Greenville. I meet Wes, Anne's husband. Anne shows me to my room. We eat a stew that has been simmering in the oven and a loaf of fresh bread. I am not used to such kindness.

"Cassandra and Clarissa are visiting your house in the country. They wanted to speak to their father about obtaining Deirdre's house," Anne says.

"Deirdre?"

"Yes, your mother-in-law." She hesitated. "Cassandra loved her and would like to perhaps make a home out of her house."

"Yes, I remember Cassandra mentioning Deirdre in a letter," I mumble. "How did you get them to me? The letters?"

"Let's just say there was some detective work involved," Anne says and winks at Wes. "Anyway, we can all drive out there tomorrow, after breakfast."

"Do they know? Do they know I'm here?" I ask.

"No," Anne says and a worried frown covers her face. I help her clear the table and dry the dishes she washes. Wes reads the newspaper at the table and makes a comment about the weather.

"It's late," Anne says. "Feel free to shower and turn in early. And, remember, we'll do this together tomorrow." She approaches me and holds me close but not tight as if she is afraid I will break.

I get my nightgown and head to the bathroom. I turn on the shower and step in. The water is hot and beats at my skin but it is not soothing. Something is wrong. There is something I need to do, but I cannot put my finger on it. I dry, put my day-time clothes back on, and head to the kitchen. Anne is filling a coffee pot with water. "For tomorrow," she says and looks at me. "What is it? Is something wrong?"

"Where are they? The girls? Are they staying here? It's getting late." I wring my hands.

"I'm not sure," Anne says. "It is late, but they are together. Let's not worry."

"Take me there. Now."

"What are you talking about?" Anne asks. "It's dark. They haven't called, but they will come back. Please, get some rest. Tomorrow will be a better time to meet them."

"Please, something is not right. I can't explain it, but we must go. Now!"

Wes and Anne look at each other and then grab their coats. We drive through Greenville and down the dusty road to the house where my two daughters are visiting their father, my husband of so long ago. Memories over-whelm me along with a sense of danger I cannot explain. We pass the church. A solitary car is parked behind it. We pass Deirdre's house. It is overgrown with weeds.

"Please, hurry!" I tell Wes.

Wes turns into the driveway and jerks to a stop. The headlights from the car connect with the eyes of a man. The house, surrounded with brush, covered with vines and grime, looms large behind him. He is young, he is angry, he is carrying two gas cans. I leap from the car and run towards him as smoke swirls from the sides of the house.

·•◆◆◆•·

What happened next is a nightmare—death and destruction soon followed by family secrets uncovered. I find myself in bed at Wes and

Anne's. She has given me something to help me sleep and tells me everything will be okay and that Cassandra and Clarissa are hospitalized.

"Who did this?" I ask.

"Local boy, trouble-maker," she says.

A cup of coffee, eggs and bacon do a lot for a shattered soul. I dress slowly and wonder for the millionth time if I can do this. We drive to the hospital. No words are spoken. We walk the halls to Room 224. Anne takes me by the hand and, again, I feel acceptance.

"Would you like to come in with us or wait?" she asks.

"I'll wait," I answer and realize how exhausted I am.

I stand outside the room and lean against the wall for support. I hear my daughter's voices—lovely woman voices. I want to melt, disappear, run, but I also want to stay and see and talk. My heart skips a beat when I hear Anne's voice coming from the hospital room, "Someone is here to meet you." And, then, there are footsteps coming towards me, and Clarissa, my eldest, says, "Mom?" She reaches for me; I have no words. I cannot stop staring at her. She pulls me into the room and I see my other little girl, now a woman, Cassandra. She is beautiful. She studies me; her eyes are wide in disbelief. Clarissa gently pushes me to Cassandra's bedside. Anne nods reassuringly. I reach out to my child. She tentatively places the tips of her fingers in the palm of my hand.

"Please forgive me," I say.

She says nothing and removes her fingertips. I hang my head; I cannot stop the flood of tears.

Weeks pass. I have been reunited with my daughters, and, yet no one is speaking. What I have yearned for, and according to Anne Christiansen, what Cassandra has yearned for—to be together—is not happening. There is bitterness. I can feel it. I have failed them, especially Cassandra, the one I left behind. I recall some of the words from the banner at the church from Romans about *nothing, nothing being able to separate us from the love of Jesus Christ*. I know that this is all I have right now. But, because this is all I have, it is also all I need. With this "love," there has to be hope.

---

I return to work, to my church and pastor. I pray. I tremble uncontrollably at times. Few things in life breed misery more than insecurity. I have a tremor in my soul that is impossible to still. I had been insecure as a child. As an adult, I wasn't doing any better. I had spent time looking for it in the wrong places—my friends, Claude, Henry. Because I was looking in the wrong places, I had failed to focus on the simple verse, *Fear not, I am with thee.*

Anne calls and tells me that Cassandra has requested a visit. *Please come*, she says. I am hopeful. Anne by-passes her house and drives me to the little country church, a hundred yards or so, from what used to be our home.

"There's someone you need to meet," she explains. We walk into the church. Sunlight filters in through stained glass windows leaving colorful patterns across the pews and center aisle. An elderly man dressed in a worn suit lumbers towards us.

"So, you're Cassandra's mother," he says. His face is timeworn and yet his eyes twinkle. "Please, come into my office?" As we settle, I hear Anne singing *What a Friend We Have in Jesus* in the sanctuary. I sit and place my hands on my knees to stop the shaking. "Your daughter, Cassandra? Lovely girl, strong girl," he says. He brings his large frame to the edge of his chair, places his forearms on his desk and stares at me. "Mrs. Walwyn, or may I call you Jacqueline?" He waits; I nod. "Our little congregation and especially our organist, Anne, have been praying for your family for years. Years…." He shakes his head as if even he cannot believe this. "It seems our prayers are being answered."

"Cassandra hasn't spoken to me," I say.

"I'm aware of this. But, she did ask you to return. Right?"

"I'm not worthy…." I start.

"I have to disagree with you," Pastor Jason says. "None of us are worthy. That is, unless we are in Christ. God's grace has made this possible."

"I don't know about any of this. The girls were baptized here. I know I need to know, but I don't."

He looks at me, puzzled.

"I went to Sunday school," I say and then feel silly. I am a middle-aged, worn-out woman. Sunday school was a life-time ago.

Pastor Jason smiles and asks, "What do you remember from Sunday School?"

"Fear not, I am with thee," I say. I feel like a child. Such a simple answer.

"For now, that is everything you need to know." He states this quietly as if it is the first time these words came from his lips. He stands, walks awkwardly to my chair, and offers his hand. I give him mine, and we walk to the sanctuary. He gets on his knees in front of the cross, uneasily, as if bearing a heavy burden. I do the same and look up. There is a carved image of a man, hands and feet pierced with nails, bleeding. I notice the tears staining his cheeks, and I remember so long ago wiping my own blood and tears with my apron the night I slit my own wrist. Pastor Jason is praying. I listen.

"Dear God. We experience such great difficulties, at times." He clears his throat as if searching for words. "May we recall your words, *Fear not, I am with thee*, as we go forward." He stops, again, as if he is tired. "With your love supporting us and your hand leading us… things will work out."

Pastor Jason rises before the *Amen* and lumbers back to his office. I hear a heavy sigh. I stay, bowed, hands folded, wondering what I am to do. Scanning my surroundings, I spot the baptismal font where my daughters were baptized so many years ago and it hits me—the fact that Cassandra and Clarissa *are God's children*. I feel the unworthiness inside me leave. Like a vapor it drifts to the cross and drops at Jesus' feet. Feeling empty and new at the same time, I hear the door open in the back of the church. Soft footsteps approach the altar. Someone is beside me, on her knees, her hand upturned, her fingers slightly curved. Her shoulder touches mine. "Don't be afraid, Mom," Cassandra says ever-so-softly; "we'll do this together." I place my fingertips in her palm. Her fingers curl over mine.

I look into her soft, gentle face, and I know the road ahead will not be easy. I can't imagine what her life has been like. How will I ever explain my own? Somehow, somehow, as I look at this man on the cross, this man called Jesus, I know that God's grasp on my life is stronger than anything, and I need not fear.

# Ramona's Visitor

Ramona's head rested on the back of her favorite chair, her eyes closed. A daily devotional booklet, a thinking-of-you card from a close friend, a recent picture of the latest great grandchild—a little girl christened Lilly—were on a lampstand within arm's reach. Beginning to doze, she was startled by an urgent rapping on her open door.

"What's a nice girl like you doing in a place like this?" someone called out.

She sat up in her chair and turned to the man filling her doorway. Dressed in pressed khakis, a polo shirt and loafers, he was clean shaven, and his haircut a recent style. She determined he might be in his late forties or early fifties. She waited.

"What's a nice girl like you doing in a place like this?" he repeated flamboyantly, his arms gesturing this way and that.

She had heard him the first time; her hearing aids had been recently checked. Unduly confident and a bit too loud, the man was beginning to amuse her. It was not unusual for someone to walk into her room. It was typically someone from church, someone who worked at Titus Assisted Living, or another resident. Each was typically quiet, reserved, and always respectful. Even the small children who occasionally visited were rehearsed before they entered the building as to the proper behavior and voice level. She wasn't sure who this person was but he oozed with friendliness and reminded her of someone….

She turned away from him. Outside the window, thin wispy strands of light grey filled the sky. A change in the weather? She wondered. After careful consideration, she shifted in her chair to face him and replied, "Well, I'm seeking God."

He rubbed his hands together, started to speak, and then stopped.

Voices from the hallway turned his attention to an elderly man hobbling by with a cane, his shoes squeaking with each meticulous step. Down the hall, several aged ladies sat at a card table, jabbering, their arthritic fingers curled around their cards.

"Here?" he questioned gruffly and threw his hands up in the air. He needed to change the subject. Rubbing his freshly shaved jawline, he reflected on his daydreaming during the car ride to Titus Assisted Living. A new car, a bigger house, maybe even an exotic vacation could be possibilities if everything worked out. He was ready to put his purposeless, dull life behind him. The broken relationships, a potential job promotion given to another less deserving, living beyond his means and the financial stress it caused had become more than he could handle.

"Of course, here." The corners of Ramona's mouth turned up exposing pearly white teeth. Her eyes twinkled as she repeated the word with emphasis, "Here!"

"Good luck!" he replied and laughed, a tone of sarcasm wiggling in.

"Good luck, not needed," she quickly replied and chuckled, too, but the laughter was of a different kind—more like a school girl's light-hearted giggle.

Without being asked, he settled himself in a wooden, straight-backed chair beside her, placed his forearms on his knees, and twiddled his thumbs. *How do you speak to someone you really don't know,* he wondered.

She deliberated. He looked familiar and yet she could not place him. Or, was it possible he was someone's long lost relative and ended up in the wrong room with the wrong elderly person? … Without knowing why, she decided to keep him interested.

"He's everywhere, you know," Ramona continued the conversation.

"Who? Who's everywhere?" He sat upright, turned toward the door and then the window.

"God," Ramona replied patiently. "We were talking about God weren't we?"

He looked about the room: a single bed covered with a quilt in pastel colors, a kitchen sink, a mini microwave, a single-cup coffee brewer, a TV in the corner with a writing desk a step away, a closet with little inside, a bathroom, and one door leading to the hallway—standing wide-open. An awareness of his own mortality along with a sense of urgency invaded his sensitivities. His eyes returned to the window and the clouds pasted beyond, a glimmer of sunlight sneaking through. Memories of his childhood surfaced: sunshine warming his back at a fishing hole, running through puddles after a rainstorm, a litter of kittens discovered in the shanty behind the house.

"That sky; beautiful, isn't it? It greets me every morning with something new," she said.

"I see that," he agreed. He looked at his watch. This was taking longer than he thought.

"It's the view from my window and then the smell of bacon drifting down the hallway," Ramona stated so softly that he could barely hear her. He looked at her side profile— still radiating beauty, peace, and contentment. She was reflecting, deeply, and he questioned the transition from a beautiful sky to bacon drifting down the hall.

"I feel energized every day," she continued. "Vince tried to protect us all last night when the sirens sounded and the storm hit. Such a good feeling to know someone wants to take care of us."

"You had storms?" he asked.

"One gentleman calls me, 'Honey,' and holds my hand when we walk," Ramona continued. "Companionship is essential in life; everybody needs it, although some don't think so."

Her guest raised his eyebrows a notch or two.

"The laundry lady touches my shoulder gently as she takes and then returns clean-smelling clothes, neatly folded. ...Always reminds me of the smell of clothes after hanging them outside on a day filled with sunshine and a soft breeze. I had the best sleep on those nights. The sheets smelled like fresh air."

Her visitor remembered his own mother hanging out the laundry on a clothesline and how he used to run under everything, feeling like he could fly. He cleared his throat; it was time to get down to business. But, Ramona was not interested.

"A friend recently took me out for ice cream; we giggled like school girls. I remember...." She stopped to take a breath, closed her eyes. It was her naptime and she was drowsy.

He was puzzled with her thought processes, and the word *dementia* creeped into his own. Knowing he had to say something, anything, and without giving it much thought, he blurted, "What's God got to do with any of this?"

She smiled and replied, "Everything! Everything…. I have found myself here at this stage of life and so it is here that I am seeking God." Ramona placed her hand over his as it rested on the chair arm and ended their conversation with three words. "Someday you'll understand."

He sat for a while, her withered hand resting on his, as she slumbered. Her fingertips cool, his palm sweaty, he soon felt more at ease. His mother had taken him to church as a child and prayed with him before he fell asleep each night. But, that was the God of his childhood. There didn't seem to be a place for God in his adult world in spite of his mother's prayers.

He had promised her a couple of years ago he would visit her sister, his Aunt Ramona. Soon after this promise, his mother, Bernice, was diagnosed with cancer and lived but a few months. His mother had indicated there may be inheritance money from his aunt. He had been a child when he last saw this aunt and here he was a grown-up, not remembering her at all. This lady did not even resemble his mother. She was small of stature; his mother was tall and big boned.

He was torn. Should he stay? He had a work evaluation meeting tomorrow morning with his manager and needed to head back; however, if there was an inheritance coming his way, he needed to know. He couldn't afford to take the time to make another trip. He pulled his hand from underneath her soft touch. Startled, she awoke.

"You're still here?" she asked. She removed her glasses and rubbed her eyes before putting them back on. "How nice. It's almost coffee time."

"Do you remember your sister, Bernice?" he tried. Maybe, this would prompt her mind, help her remember family and any obligations she might have to him.

"Bernice? A sister?" Ramona looked puzzled. He nodded his affirmation, gaining confidence. "A sister would have been nice. Had brothers. All deceased by now."

"Are you sure?" he struggled. Why was it so hard to get this old lady to remember a sister?

"Of course, I'm sure." She pushed herself to the edge of the chair and stood. "Let's get coffee. You'll feel better soon."

Frustrated, he walked beside her and her walker to the dining area where coffee, tea, and cookies were served. Others sat around tables covered with plastic tablecloths. Some had adult bibs covering their shirts. Quiet conversations about the weather, family members, and the upcoming holiday bounced about.

Ramona tugged on his shirt sleeve. "I'm sorry, but I don't know your name," she confessed. "I'd like to introduce you to the others."

"It's James," he replied. "James Freeman. You *know* my mother." Ramona's eyes rolled from one side to the other and then to the top of her head.

"James?" she asked. "James means *supplanter*, one who follows. Bet you didn't know that."

"No, guess I didn't," he replied, annoyed and losing patience. The minute hand on the large white-faced clock tick-tocked in the dining area.

"Ramona means *protector*. Funny, isn't it, little person like me with a name that means that," she mused.

"Freeman, my last name is Freeman," James stated. He looked at his watch, his stomach growled; he had given up lunch to make this trip.

"You're irritated with me, aren't you?" Ramona asked. "I can usually tell. Been around a long time, you know."

"No, it's fine. I just wanted you to know my last name, Freeman," he said, rubbed his temples with his fingertips, and imagined eating a cheese burger and fries on the way out of town.

Her forehead wrinkled and she looked up at the ceiling. Seconds later, she set her coffee cup down with a clunk and grabbed his hand. "I'm so sorry, James! We've been waiting for your visit." He sat up straighter, relaxed his shoulders. *Finally*, he thought and breathed deeply, she remembered. She pulled a tissue from her sleeve and wiped a tear from her eye.

"I'm relieved you remember," he replied, chose two cookies from the tray, and took a bite from the peanut butter one.

"*Your* aunt, my good friend, Ramona Freeman, who shared my first name, lived just down the hall." Ramona pulled her tissue out again and wiped another tear and blew her nose. "How I miss her. I'm so sorry…. She passed. It's been a year or more. I guess no one told you."

An expletive escaped from his lips, he stammered a *sorry*, and choked on his chocolate chip cookie. The others looked at him and tried to determine what kind of character this man was. By the time he gulped his coffee and both cookies, he had developed a headache. This whole day had been a waste of time. Why hadn't he come sooner? Or, why did he bother to come at all? He had more pressing issues than spending time with some silly old woman and her odd ideas.

"I'm sorry you missed seeing your aunt," Ramona sympathized. "But, I'm so glad you came. Your picture sat on her dresser, and she often spoke of you, thinking you might stop by. Strange isn't it, how time passes so quickly." He said nothing; he really felt quite worn out. In fact, he was ticked.

"I just don't understand," he lamented to himself with a head shake.

"There's always a greater purpose at work," Ramona replied, herself not really understanding James' behavior. He stood and wiped cookie crumbs from his shirt.

"Thanks for the visit and the coffee," he said with as much sincerity as he could muster. Her arms reached out to him. Awkwardly, he leaned above her to accept the hug bringing him at eye level with the others at the table. Each one gazed at him, a thoughtful look of curiosity and fellowship, a wink or two. The hug felt good. It reminded him of his mother's arms, her scent, her warmth. He lingered.

"You come back, now," Ramona whispered in his ear, "and don't wait for so long."

He left Titus Assisted Living as the sun rested brilliant in the west, the clouds rimmed with orange and pink. He thought about time passing quickly, so quickly. He wanted to kick himself for a missed opportunity. He thought about Ramona, the place she lived, and the others.

Sliding into the car and feeling older than when he had arrived, he realized he had left his key inside Titus Assisted Living. Grumbling, James got out of the car, slammed the door, and returned to the building. Once inside, he heard Ramona's voice above all the others. He took a few steps and peered around the corner to see the table where he had been sitting. Ramona and the others, heads bowed, hands holding each other, were in prayer. He eavesdropped.

"We are here together, Lord, thankful that you have given us another day to feel purposeful, to care for others," Ramona spoke loudly so everyone could hear. "James visited today. But,You know that…." James lingered and watched a few nod their heads in agreement. "He's a good man. Just needs a little encouragement. You bring him back when You're ready. Yes, we know we got business to finish. Thy will be done."

With the *Amen*, James realized the key had been in his back pocket all along and quietly slipped out of the building, inquisitive and aware that there was possibly more to his life than he had previously thought. Starting his car, he took the exit from Titus Assisted Living and read the inscription on the sign, *Cast all your cares upon Him, for He cares for you*. Examining himself in the rearview mirror, he blurted out loud and without much thought, "You don't realize the mess I've created for myself."

With a tight grasp on the steering wheel, he realized that when he woke up tomorrow morning, his world would be much the same as it was today. It had been convenient, even self-serving, to blame others and even God for his circumstances. The word *tomorrow* was both troublesome and hopeful. An image of aging folks, hands attached in prayer, came to mind. Along with Ramona's words, "James visited today. But, You know that….He's a good man. Just needs a little encouragement. You bring him back when You're ready. Yes, we know we got business to finish. Thy will be done."

James took his time on his way home, his perceptions beginning to shift.

# HOPE

The phone sitting on the kitchen counter rang, once, twice, three times before stopping. Bonnie frowned at her husband and doubted that he would get up from his Lazy-Boy chair to answer it. Hank sat with his feet up, remote control in his hand, searching for a television western he hadn't already seen. *Bonanza, Gunsmoke, The Rifleman, Wagon Train*, they all ran together for her although she always had a fancy for Little Joe from *Bonanza*. It wouldn't hurt him to get a little exercise once in a while, she thought; although, it was after ten, and no one who knew them would call at this hour. She put her journal down and headed for the bathroom when the phone rang again. Once, twice.... She rolled her eyes and headed for the kitchen.

"Hello?" she answered on the third ring.

"Ah, yes, is this the Hank Bergholtz residence?" The caller was female, a little breathless.

"Yes," Bonnie said and thought about hanging up.

"You must be Bonnie." The voice was sweet and chummy. When Bonnie said nothing, the woman continued. "You *are* Hank's wife, aren't you?"

"Yes," Bonnie answered, impatient. "Who's calling?"

"I was in your husband's graduating class. I'm *sure* he remembers me. But, it's you I want to talk to tonight. You've published a book, right?"

"Yes," Bonnie answered, hooked.

"I read it. *Tangled Web*? It's really quite good. Have you been writing for a while?"

Bonnie stood straighter and grabbed a pencil off the counter before answering. "It's my first book although I've been scribbling notes for years in a journal."

"Well, I saw it on the internet, recognized the last name, and thought you might be Hank's wife." Bonnie waited. *Who is the tall, dark stranger there? Maverick is the name....* grew louder and louder from the television. Bonnie covered the phone mouthpiece.

"Hank, turn that down!"

"I ordered it from Amazon," the female continued. "Couldn't put it down. I hope you don't mind that I entered it in a competition for you."

"A competition?" Bonnie asked and considered .... *Just maybe I'll get the recognition I deserve.*

"I hope you don't mind," the woman continued.

"No. I guess not," Bonnie replied. "Who is this?"

"Hope Claude," the voice said. "And, congratulations! You've won an award from the Iowa Women's Press Association."

------ ·•✦•✦•· ------

If you're familiar with the movie *Misery*, and the actress Cathy Bates, you're in the right mind-set. If you're not, think Alfred Hitchcock, and you're getting there; and although Bonnie wrote works of fiction, please remember that truth *is* stranger than fiction.

A couple of weeks later on a Friday late afternoon, Bonnie left her husband with a hamburger casserole in the oven, stashed a few things in the backseat of their worn-out Rambler, and headed to Hope's home. A sense of excitement, a heightened awareness of possibilities caused her fingers to quiver on the steering wheel. She would be staying over-night with Hope, and they would travel together to Council Bluffs where the Iowa Women's Press Association Executive Board would be meeting on Saturday. The organization, according to Hope, would present Bonnie with an award for her novel.

On the way to Fort Raven, Bonnie daydreamed. She imagined a light supper with Hope and some girl talk before a leisurely shower and a good night's sleep in a carefully decorated guest room. After all, Hope had explained to Bonnie that she was a popular journalist for the well-reputed Fort Raven *Messenger*. Known for her human interest articles, she featured persons, pets, or situations that evoked others' interest, sympathy or motivations. It seemed fitting that such a person would live in a nice home, possibly Victorian, with a wraparound porch, arched entryways to each room, plush carpeting, a fireplace in a bedroom or two. Perhaps there would be tea or hot chocolate before bedtime. Bonnie envisioned Hope Claude's article, *Up and Coming Author wins IWPA Award*, in the *Messenger*. The personal interest article would have details on their weekend together, all bringing more attention to Bonnie Bergholtz's name and her book, *Tangled Web*. The entire weekend could change her life!

Realizing she was within twenty minutes of arrival time, Bonnie pulled her cell phone from her purse and punched in Hope's number to clarify directions to the house. No one answered. Although she had never met Hope Claude, they had emailed each other about the IWPA book competition and a few details concerning the weekend agenda. When Bonnie had asked Hank, her husband, about Hope, his classmate, he had shrugged his shoulders.

"What's her maiden name?" he had asked.

"There couldn't have been too many girls named Hope in your class, Hank," she answered pretentiously.

"You're probably right," Hank had mumbled, looked out the kitchen window at the livestock needing to be fed, and dressed in his usual chore clothes, started to the back door. Bonnie heard his last words before he stepped outside, "Can't remember Hope's last name. Can't even remember what she looked like."

Several miles later, Bonnie punched re-dial. Someone picked up, breathing heavily.

"Hope?" Bonnie asked. "Are you okay?"

"You're here?" Hope sounded nervous. "Already?"

"No, about fifteen minutes away."

"Oh. I've been cleaning, and I don't have any food." Hope panted. Bonnie didn't know what she expected. "There's a McDonald's down the street from my house," Hope suggested.

"Oh. Would you like me to get you something?" Bonnie offered.

"Sure, great idea. I'll have a cheeseburger, fries, and a soda. Make it large."

Bonnie parked at McDonalds', used the restroom, and placed a large order for Hope and a plain cheeseburger for herself. She took her time driving the final three blocks to Hope's house. She found Shadow Street and Hope's house number painted on a bent-over, rusty mailbox, #9.

One dim street light stood at the end of the block. The houses were worn-out, small, cottage-like, and surrounded by prehistoric perennials. Disappointed, Bonnie unplugged the Garmin, gathered her over-night bag from the back of the car, and grabbed the McDonalds' order. Outside the car, wet fall leaves muffled every step. A wire gate attached to a fallen fence line confronted her. Stepping over the barrier, Bonnie side-tracked the cracked sidewalk and approached the house. A broken light fixture hung next to the door. Raising her hand to ring a doorbell, Bonnie stopped in mid-air.

An open doorway framed an exhausted-looking woman. She was about five feet tall and built like a marshmallow. Wire-rimmed glasses hung over the tip of her nose and perspiration dripped down the sides of her face. A few gray-spattered curls were damp with sweat and plastered to her forehead.

"Hope?" Bonnie asked but wondered if it was perhaps Hope's mother, or sister, or possibly a neighbor?

"You came alone?" Hope asked, and Bonnie turned to see who else she might be expecting.

"Sure," Bonnie answered although she was not. Hope scrutinized Bonnie over her glasses, said nothing, took the McDonald's bag, turned, and started to eat a hamburger on the way to the kitchen.

Settling herself at a small table, she dumped the rest of the contents of the McDonalds' order on the table and ate fries in handfuls. Bonnie placed her overnight bag against the wall, took off her coat, and pulled out the remaining chair. Also on the table was a 1970 Clay Central Yearbook opened to a page of senior class pictures and plastered with fingerprints. As Bonnie unwrapped her cheeseburger, she scanned the pictures until her eyes fell on the photo of Hank Bergholtz, her husband. He looked good back then, she thought, in spite of the finger smudges.

"I'm sorry, but I'm exhausted from cleaning the house," Hope said, her mouth still full.

"Oh, please don't apologize. You didn't have to go to so much trouble," Bonnie said. The woman seemed rattled, unsettled, uncomfortable. "You and Hank graduated from the same class?" Bonnie asked trying to ease the awkwardness.

"Oh, yes," Hope said, flipped the page, and pointed to a young woman by the name of Hope Hoover. "That's me," she stated emphatically. A young woman dressed in a gold sweater with an attached white, lace collar stared directly at the camera. A smirk, dark brown eyes, and short pixie haircut completed the picture.

Not able to see any resemblance, Bonnie studied the photo and noted that a small black heart was inked in on the left side of her sweater. Seeing that Hope was waiting for a reaction, she responded, "Wow. Long time ago, right?"

Hope stared at her briefly, as if insulted by her response.

"We have an early morning tomorrow," she said, finished the fries, and wiped her hands on the front of her faded, plaid blouse. "We should probably call it a day. Plus, I disconnected the cable from the television. It was sending out weird messages; got rid of it."

"Weird messages? What do you mean?" Bonnie asked.

"Have you ever communicated with someone through the television?" Hope's question came out slowly and with a pause between each word.

"Uh, I'm not sure I know what you mean," Bonnie replied.

When Hope dropped her chin and peered at her over her glasses, Bonnie quickly answered, "No, I never have." And, then, curious, "Is someone trying to send you messages?"

"Someone I used to know," Hope replied, got up from the table, and opened the refrigerator. Leftover takeout containers, a wrinkled apple, and dirty dishes filled it to the brim. It was obvious that Hope had stashed everything left on her kitchen counter into it when doing her so-called cleaning. Pulling a partial package of Oreos from a shelf on the door, Hope offered Bonnie a cookie. Bonnie shook her head and held up the back of her hand to her nose to prevent her eyes from watering.

"Haven't had time to get groceries. Guess we don't need them. Follow me. I'll show you to your room."

Bonnie picked up the McDonald's wrappers and looked for a wastepaper basket.

"Leave it on the table," Hope said. "Garbage is all outside."

Bonnie followed Hope out of the kitchen and down a short hallway. The house was small, one story, consisting of a tiny kitchen, a living room with a large blank television screen and two upholstered chairs, one bedroom, one storeroom, and a bathroom. Bonnie realized she was being taken to the only bedroom in the house. It was immaculate. A white coverlet lay across the bed; huge pillows stood against a Walnut headboard. A framed picture of Hope and an older man stood on the dresser.

"Please, don't give up your room," Bonnie said. "Where will you and your husband sleep?"

"Deceased," she said. "Ed's dead." Hope took the picture, opened a top drawer of the dresser and stuffed it inside, upside down.

"Oh, I'm sorry. I didn't know," Bonnie responded.

"No worries," Hope said. "I'll take the couch. It'll be a short night." She closed the bedroom door behind her. Bonnie looked around, part of her expecting to hear a lock clicked from the other side. Even though she didn't feel that she was in danger, she felt a nagging sense of something peculiar.

The house was quiet. Wanting less light, Bonnie switched on the bedside lamp and turned off the overhead light. There were two windows covered with heavy curtains. Under the heavy drapes were blackout shades. She checked to see if there was a lock on the inside of the door. None. Quickly, she undressed and pulled a nightgown over her head. Shivering, she studied the items on Hope's dresser—a brush and comb matching set rested on a lace doily, a dried flower arrangement lay on a hand mirror. A pink, ceramic heart container sat on another doily. Bonnie carefully removed the lid to find a 1970 Clay Central class ring cushioned in a tissue.

Although she wanted to, she dared not peek into the closet or open the dresser drawers. The bed was impeccably made, and she longed to crawl under the creamy-white sheets. Instead, she selected a pillow, gathered a quilt at the end of the bed, pulled her knees up, and wrapped herself tightly as an October wind pulled at the windows. Closing her eyes and trying to relax, she soon heard the sound of static creeping under the bedroom door. A man's razor? A small power tool? Hope had mentioned the television did not work. Bonnie remembered that Hope said she communicated with someone from her past through the television. The sound of static was soon replaced by the wailing wind outside and a banging—a lose shutter?

The clock ticked midnight when Bonnie, an ache crawling up the backside of her head, climbed out of bed, and dug in her overnight bag for aspirin. Wanting a drink of water, needing to go to the bathroom, she opened the bedroom door and stopped. A round figure was sitting in the opposite room, the storage room, with its back to the door. Surrounded by boxes stacked to the ceiling at odd angles and looking as if they could topple in on her, Hope hovered over a large computer and typed wildly.

"Hope?" Bonnie broke the dark. Hope jerked her hands off the keyboard and turned slowly, the only light in the room coming from the computer screen behind her.

"Everything all right?" Bonnie asked.

"Oh. Just finishing an article for the *Messenger*. Due tomorrow," Hope explained and trained her eyes on Bonnie. The word *procrastinator* crossed Bonnie's mind. On the other hand, was this possibly an article about the IWPA awards to be given tomorrow? Her curiosity got the best of her.

"What's it about?"

Hope made an exaggerated look at the watch on her right wrist and slid her eyes up Bonnie's frame—starting at her bare feet and not stopping until she got to the top of her head.

Bonnie covered one foot with the other and touched her hair wondering what Hope was seeing. "Sorry, to bother you; I need to use the bathroom," she mumbled and rushed to the bathroom, locking the door behind her.

Within minutes, Bonnie returned to the computer glow spilling out into the hallway—and forced herself not to make eye contact with this stranger whose bed she was sleeping in. Once in the bedroom, she found a chair and hooked the backside under the doorknob. Sitting on the edge of the bed, she thought about her husband, but knew he would not answer at this time of the night. Hank would be sound asleep in an upstairs bedroom. Besides that, what would she say? Bonnie visualized him snoring, his graying hair in clumps, smelling of beer and chips, and happy to have a weekend to himself. It seemed that his only interests were watching television, getting the outdoor chores done, and checking the daily mail before he turned it over to her to pay the bills and attend to the business side of their marriage.

With bitterness taking a foothold, she fell asleep. Silly and odd dreams leaked into the night—her wedding day with gray stains appearing on her white dress with no one else in the church but her. Another, with her in elementary school falling from a slide, the laughter of children filling the air. And, then a KNOCK, KNOCK as the bedroom doorknob twisted and turned.

"Time to go," Hope sang out.

Bonnie pulled herself out of bed, removed the chair and opened the door. There stood Hope looking rested and excited dressed in a multicolored blouse and palazzo pants, a smear of garish lipstick across her lips, the front of her hair spiked. Bonnie rubbed her eyes and looked at the clock. 5 a.m.

"Ready?" Hope chirped.

"Give me a few minutes," Bonnie croaked, her throat dry, her eyes grainy. She hurriedly dressed in slacks and a sweater and slipped on comfortable pumps. After a quick stop in the bathroom to brush her teeth and apply a little makeup, she grabbed a notebook and her purse, and followed Hope down the hallway, noting that static electricity had morphed her into a colorful ball.

Outside, fall air swirled the leaves on the ground. Bonnie wished she had brought a jacket and wondered how Hope could stay warm in her jersey, summery outfit. However, the cool air cleared her head, and she was hopeful that this day would end well.

"Do you need the GPS? We can use mine," Bonnie offered.

"Oh my goodness, of course not," Hope said flippantly. "I've been to Council Bluffs many times. Hop in."

With a cough or two the van engine rumbled to life, catapulted out of the driveway, down Shadow Avenue, and headed out of Fort Raven on a gravel road.

"Did you want to get on the main highway?" Bonnie questioned. Hope's headlights seemed dim and the sun hadn't yet sparked the horizon as the van blasted through a stop sign. Bonnie checked the security of her seat belt, took some deep breaths, and convinced herself that this lady had no sinister plan. Hope was simply odd. After all, she was a journalist with a worthy job for the *Messenger*.

Bonnie breathed easier when she spotted freeway traffic in the distance, and Hope took the proper exit and blended in with early morning commuters. She tried conversations with Hope about her work as a journalist. Hope gave yes or no answers and no details. Remembering the picture on the dresser in the bedroom, Bonnie brought up another topic.

"The photo that was on your dresser?" Bonnie said. "...very nice picture of you and your husband. How long ago was it taken?"

"You mean of Ed and me?" Hope asked.

"Yes. Ed was your husband?"

"Was? Still is. In the nursing home," she replied.

"I thought he was ____...." Bonnie could not say the word "dead."

"Dead?" Hope said it for her. "Oh heavens, why would I say that!"

Perspiration pricked Bonnie's armpits, spine, and forehead. She shivered. Her cell phone lay at the bottom of her purse. Who would she call? What would she say? *I'm with a crazy lady and I'm not sure what to do.* She looked inside the passing cars to focus on something else besides her anxieties until Hope speeded up to over eighty miles an hour. Bonnie gripped the sides of her seat and said nothing as the telephone poles whipped past.

"I need gas," Hope eventually said. "Plus, we need a bite to eat." She took an exit with the promise of a Casey's.

"Get me some breakfast pizza and a coffee," Hope ordered as she pumped gas. Bonnie walked into Casey's thankful for a reprieve from Hope and the brown van. She pulled two slices of sausage and egg pizza from a hot turntable and filled two Styrofoam cups with black coffee. At the counter, she handed the clerk her credit card and wondered about leaving a note. Something like, *If I'm found missing, Hope Claude may be responsible.* But, that's silly, she thought; I am going to the IWPA to receive an award for my book, *Tangled Web.* The fact that she traveled with an unpredictable woman was immaterial.

Hope wolfed down the pizza, crumpled the sack it came in, and tossed it in the backseat.

"Gotta any cream, sugar?" she asked Bonnie.

"No," Bonnie answered leaving out the *sorry* she would have offered to any other person.

Bonnie finished her own slice of pizza and flipped the litter in the backseat, caring no longer about making a good impression on this woman. Greasy pizza and Styrofoam coffee—something she would normally not eat or drink—surprisingly revived her, and she tried to put on her positive thinking cap. During the next hour or so, there was little conversation as Hope drove somewhat erratically over and sometimes way under the speed limit. Bonnie watched the sun rise, noticed the countryside, listened to the whine of the wheels, and, then, thought of Hank. He would be getting ready to do the farm chores; she wondered if he missed her. Taking a deep breath, she imagined receiving the award for her book, a book he never asked about, a creative part of her life he showed no interest in.

Sighing heavily, she asked Hope, "When the awards are presented, will I be expected to say anything?"

"Oh, no, nothing like that," Hope muttered, a burp popping out.

Not trusting Hope's thinking, Bonnie considered a few words and phrases that might be appropriate. It was during these musings that she realized the exit for Council Bluffs was just ahead. She mouthed a *Thank God*, a mere expression of relief. Hope took the exit, turned right, and headed down Walton Street for a mile or so before jerking to a stop.

"I don't recognize any of this." She admitted. "It's supposed to be at a church, and I haven't seen one yet."

"There's a church," Bonnie said. Seeing a steeple rise above the other buildings several blocks away, they headed in that direction and pulled into a parking lot filled with cars. A sign, "Food bank open today," was posted.

"Not the right one," Hope stated.

"We can ask for directions," Bonnie suggested. Begrudgingly, Hope pulled to a closer parking space and they both got out of the car. Bonnie no longer trusted Hope with anything. A gentleman met them at a side door, a bag of groceries under one arm. Dressed in faded, baggy jeans, and a ragged t-shirt, he kept his head down.

"Excuse me, Sir." Bonnie stopped him. "We're looking for the New Covenant Church." Hope stood mutely, her glasses on the tip of her nose and boring her eyes first on Bonnie and then on the man with a bag of groceries.

"Don't have no paper or pen," he grumbled but started to explain, gesturing with his arms, the groceries tipping, a carton of milk plopping on the ground.

Bonnie grabbed paper and pen from her purse, handed it to Hope, picked up the injured carton, and offered to hold the grocery bag as he explained.

"It's only about three miles from here," he said. He pointed here and there while Hope wrote down street names and numbers. Back in the car, she handed Bonnie the directions, written in cursive loops and swirls.

They arrived at the New Covenant Church and the Iowa Women's Press Association's meeting only a few minutes late. A dozen cars were scattered on the parking lot of a large brick building. Hope took the lead, her cloth brief case bumping her legs with every step. Inside a side door, a long table with swivel, cushioned chairs and smiling faces greeted them. Names were exchanged; agendas were passed out; carafes of coffee were available. A business meeting convened with a treasurer's report, a secretary's report, old business and new business. Hope sat at the end of the table—her chin dropped to her marshmallow shape, and she snored softly. The others smiled at Bonnie, as if *she's your friend*.... And Bonnie thought *if you only knew*. Although Bonnie attempted to show some interest in their agenda, she had no prior knowledge of the Iowa Women's Press Association or what their purpose was. She did note on the agenda that the award presentations would be given after adjournment. So, she let her mind wander to other things and made a mental list of things needing to be done when she got home: pay the bills, call her mother, weed the flower patch, and possibly write a sequel to *Tangled Web*? The idea was not as stimulating as she thought it might be.

Bonnie heard the motion for adjournment and straightened in her chair. Hope wiggled in her seat and yawned. The presiding president haphazardly handed out large manila envelopes to each attendee stating that awards or recognition were inside along with the submission. Everyone gathered their things. The pushing back of chairs made screeching sounds on the hard, tile floor. Talk of weekend plans fluttered about. No formal presentations; no acceptance speeches necessary.

As others were making arrangements to meet at The Other Place for drinks and dinner, Bonnie sat at the table and opened the manila envelope to see her book that had been submitted months earlier by Hope. There was a certificate stating that she had earned an "honorable mention" for the novel, *Tangled Web*. Really, she thought. I came all this way for an honorable mention with no presentation, no recognition? Judge's comments were written in a strangely familiar cursive and signed with a man's name.

*This was a nice attempt by a beginning author. However, the male protagonist's appeal was not truly developed. The book lacked a compelling theme and had a frustrating conclusion. You may want to attend a writers' conference.... I wish you the best with future projects.*

*Jake Fulsome*

Bonnie read it several times and felt ill. *Such comments are not deserving of an honorable mention* was her first thought. Her second thought—*this is not a man's handwriting.* Her third thought—*this handwriting looks familiar. Hope's?* Her heart sinking bit by bit, she picked up the award certificate and the book to place them back in the manila envelope and realized the book's binding had not been cracked. Jack Fulsome had not read the book. Hope Claude had not read the book. Nor had anyone else.

Bonnie glared at Hope as she stuffed the day's papers in her cloth briefcase. In the parking lot, on the way to the van, Bonnie followed Hope, step by step, evil thoughts filling her head. *What was her purpose,* Bonnie wondered. *Why did she bring me all the way to Council Bluffs to an IWPA meeting, an organization I know nothing about, for such an award when the book was not even read?*

They both got in the van, doors screeching, then thudding shut. An uneasy silence permeated the atmosphere. Wheels soon whined on the pavement below. Dark clouds scuttled above; tiny snowflakes peppered the air and bounced on the windshield. Bonnie counted to ten; she did some breathing exercises; and she thought of questions to ask Hope to get some resolution to this whole, senseless mess.

"The weather, it's changing," Bonnie said and broke the interminable silence.

"Snow in the forecast. That time of year," Hope replied and fiddled with the radio. Inarticulate voices and loud static filled the car as she twisted the dial back and forth.

"Do you know the person who judged my book?" Bonnie asked raising her voice above the radio disturbance. When Hope continued to search for stations, Bonnie turned her face towards her and said loudly, "His name is Jack Fulsome."

KATHLEEN STAUFFER

Hope switched the radio off and replied, "His name is Jake, and we never know who the judges will be."

"So, you don't know him, this Jake?" Bonnie asked.

"Why do you ask?" Hope asked and stepped on the accelerator.

Noting that the brown van was hurtling way over the speed limit, Bonnie tempered her voice. "Well, the book's binding was never cracked. The book was not read by anyone," she said and gripped the sides of her seat.

"Perhaps, he had another copy," Hope said and snorted.

Bonnie leaned back against her seat, and let her eyes roam around the van. Still resting in between the seats were the directions to the church Hope had written. Bonnie pulled the judge's comments from her own manila packet and placed the directions and comments side by side. The handwriting was the same. It was obvious that the judge's comments had been written by Hope Claude, journalist for the *Messenger*.

As Hope turned off the highway, she mumbled something to herself and then chuckled. Signs indicated opportunities for gas and food. Bonnie was relieved they would be stopping and wondered if she should call Hank to come and get her. He would be confused, perhaps angry. How could she explain her dilemma over the phone when she didn't even get it herself?

Bonnie paid for two Pizza Hut buffets, Hope saying that she had left her cash at home and was starving. They sat across from each other, neither saying a word. Bonnie ate very little; Hope went back for seconds and then thirds. Bonnie kept noting the clock on the wall, eager to get home and be done with the entire weekend.

An hour later, the brown van pulled into #9, Shadow Avenue. Bonnie followed Hope into the house and quickly gathered her belongings from the bedroom. She could hear Hope in the storage room across the hall, talking to herself. Arms full, Bonnie hurried to the front door, hoping to escape without a goodbye or a thank you. However, Hope was at the door waiting…. In her hands, she held a travel cup and a t-shirt, all with the logo, the *Messenger*, imprinted on each. When she presented them to Bonnie, Bonnie's heart softened.

"Thank you," Bonnie said tentatively and not knowing what else to say and remembering the photograph on the dresser, she added, "I hope your husband is doing better."

"My husband?" Hope asked and looked at her blankly. "Ed's dead."

Confused, again, Bonnie said, "Oh, well thanks for this, this stuff," and motioned to the t-shirt and travel mug in Hope's outstretched but clutched hands.

"It's for Hank!" Hope exclaimed, a gleam in her eye. Bonnie's softened heart grew cold as Hope placed the items in her arms. She left the house without a word, her eyes downcast— walked the cracked sidewalk, stepped over the downed fence line, and tossed everything in the backseat. Pulling away from #9, Shadow Avenue, she felt tired, discouraged, and used. As she settled in for a two hour ride home, she noted a slice of moon in a black, black, sky. A wisp of wind swept through her little Rambler, and she started to cry.

———— ·+◆◆◆·+· ————

Six months later, Bonnie picked up her grocery list, left Hank with his television program, and headed east on the gravel road leading to the highway. There was never much traffic on the road in front of their farm and what there was, they usually recognized—the neighbors going to and from work, the occasional delivery truck. As she neared the stop sign, she met an oddly familiar brown van traveling at a snail's pace. The driver was hunched over the steering wheel, her glasses on the tip of her nose. Bonnie slowed and watched in the rearview mirror. The van kicked up a few dust swirls before it slowed and turned into the Bergholtz drive.

What possible explanation did Hope have for a visit? How did she even know *where* Bonnie and Hank lived?

After Bonnie's last encounter with Hope, she had no wish to ever see her again. She decided to let Hank handle it. After all, Hope had been his classmate. With blood pressure a bit elevated, she continued her trip into town and picked up the needed items. At the checkout, she crowded in front of an elderly lady already in line saying, "Sorry, it's an emergency." And then giggled, not understanding her own behavior.

She placed the few grocery bags in the back seat on top of a manila envelope which contained an honorable mention certificate and the unread book, *Tangled Web*. A coffee mug and t-shirt with the logo, the *Messenger*, lay on the floor with miscellaneous car clutter. Neither had been removed from the car since that weekend she attended the IWPA meeting in Council

Bluffs so many months ago. A meeting that Hank never asked about; an experience she never shared with anyone. Bonnie slid into the driver's seat and took her time driving the few miles to get home. When she arrived, there was no van. Relieved that Hank had sent Hope on her way, perhaps after a short conversation, or, more than likely, he hadn't even answered the door, Bonnie gathered her groceries and headed inside.

She placed the groceries on the kitchen counter and realized how very quiet it was. The television was off. Hank was not in the house. She ventured to the garage. His pickup was parked in its usual spot. She started towards the small barn and called his name, harshly at first, and, then quietly, and then not at all. Walking part way down their driveway, she turned east and then west, looking and listening –a dust roll, a rumble of an engine? Neither....

She returned to the house, took several deep breaths, and went up the steps to their bedroom. She checked the closets and drawers not knowing what she might find. She looked in the extra bedroom where their luggage was stored. All was intact. She did not know where her husband was. She did not know what happened to Hope. She moved to the bed—still unmade—drew her legs up to her chest, and wrapped her arms around them. She made herself small and started to imagine. There was no sense of dread, no wave of foreboding—only a premonition that her life was about to change.

Hope?

Minutes later, remembering the grocery bags still on the counter, probably with melting ice cream, she returned to the kitchen. Stashing items in cupboards and the freezer, she then folded the brown sacks, hearing every crackle. With an uneasy stillness infusing every crack and corner of their house, she stepped into the living room and settled in Hank's chair. Taking a deep breath, Bonnie picked up the remote and wondered what he had been watching. Pushing the power button, Iowa Public Television sprang to life with a feature on antique tractors. She switched if off. Her eyes moved to the miscellaneous newspapers and magazines layered in a basket beside his chair. Pulling the Farm Bureau Spokesman, Sports Illustrated, and copies of the local newspaper aside, she spotted a package labeled *Hank Bergholtz*, their address, and *confidential* written in familiar loops and swirls in the bottom corner. The postmark was two days before she had left for the IWPA conference with Hope, months ago. Bonnie wondered why she had never previously noticed the package.

She opened the packet to find a copy of her book, Tangled Web, with worn corners and rickety binding. She leafed through the first few pages and read the Walter Scott quote she had started the book with, *What a tangled web we weave, when first we practice to deceive…* and sighed with a familiar ache. The lack of recognition and the whole miserable weekend with Hope washed through her, again. She turned to Chapter 1 and started to read and then flipped quickly through the remainder of the book, realizing that someone had highlighted certain parts and written comments in the margins. Bonnie's skin crawled as she scanned the familiar cursive with its loops and twirls. For the past six months she'd been excusing Hope's rude and deranged behavior as the unintentional thoughtlessness of a demented old woman. In fact, it had been calculated malice. The margin notes expressed things like, *I always cared. I never stopped loving you. We need each other.* And the one that hurt most, *Bonnie never cared. She could have never loved you to have written these things.*

Overcome with angry confusion, Bonnie dug deeper in the basket. At the bottom was a 1970 Clay Central Yearbook. She opened a bookmarked page to see Hank Bergoltz's picture. Comments surrounding the photo included, *nice guy, good luck with the farm, remember the FFA trip to Kansas City?* She peered knowingly at an almost indistinguishable inked-in black heart on his suit jacket pocket. Flipping forward, she found Hope Hoover's picture; the girl with a smirk and a pixie. Under the image in familiar cursive were her words, *My favorite song—"Someday We'll Be Together."* Using her fingers, Bonnie rubbed the faint black heart inked-in on the left side of Hope's gold sweater and tried to make it disappear. It had been there for decades; it wasn't going away. Dropping both her novel and the yearbook, Bonnie felt as if she were teetering on the edge of a precipice. Outside, the day dimmed. A Federal Express truck rattled past on the gravel road and then the neighbor's pickup. Bonnie sank to the floor, pulled her knees to her chest and closed her eyes.

------ ✦✦✦✦✦ ------

Hank? An object of desire?

Bonnie sent her thoughts tunneling through the crusted layers of hurts and disappointments, back, back, through the years to a time when she'd felt proud to be Hank's girlfriend. Opening her eyes, she retrieved the yearbook and studied Hank's picture. His young face wore the goofy, charming look that used to seem so cute before Bonnie understood that light-hearted can turn into "who, me?" when the honeymoon is over and the hard work begins. All too soon, Hank's self-deprecating shrug had become his standard response to her hopes and dreams. *You want to go back to school? What are you looking at me for? You want a nicer house? I'm already working two jobs, what more do you want?* As the wedding anniversaries stumbled one upon another, the dismissive shrug devolved into a disgusted head-shake which was finally reduced to a perpetual, silent scowl.

Hope Hoover had not lived through those soul-crushing years with Hank. Her puppy-love infatuation had sailed, unblemished, through the decades to land here and now on Bonnie's doorstep. Of course, Hope's view of Hank was sheer fantasy. She didn't really know him. And yet...

Why had Hank gone with her? Where had they gone? What could Hank possibly see in Hope?

Picking herself up off the floor, Bonnie went to the kitchen for a glass of water. Searching the cabinets, she found a bottle of aspirin, shook several out, and swallowed them. The truth pressed in on her. She knew what Hank saw in Hope. He saw a woman who thought he was wonderful. Bonnie imagined the two of them, sitting together in a restaurant booth, Hope murmuring sympathetically as Hank poured out the story of his wife's selfish, ruthless ambition.

"That's not me!" The words burst from between her clenched teeth. She paced the room, her thoughts racing. *Yes, I have ambitions, but I'm not ruthless. I've supported Hank's ambitions as much as my own. I work as hard as he does to keep this farm going. And I never asked him to put me through school; I paid for that with my own earnings. I care about Hank, I want him to be happy. I just want him to care about my happiness too.*

Hearing the cattle moo and snort from the barnyard, Bonnie was reminded that there was no one to complete the evening chores. She pulled on an old coat and slipped on Hank's overshoes over her own shoes and headed out to feed the livestock. The rhythm of the work had a pleasing familiarity. *I love this farm,* she realized. *This is my home.*

In all her dreams of success as an author, she'd never thought of leaving the farm, or Hank, for more than a few days at a time. Yes, there would be book tours and writers conferences, but always, she would return to the farm. She'd even imagined Hank looking at her with new-found respect when she invested her royalties in new siding for the barn and maybe a skid-loader which would lighten his work load. And she would have converted the tool shed into her private writing studio, all pine-paneled with a picture window facing the pasture.

"I didn't want to be rid of Hank," Bonnie said softly to Rosie, her favorite cow, scratching behind her ears and rubbing her muzzle. "I just wanted him to like me, the real me, including my creative side."

Her daydreams held no comfort now. They no longer rested in the safe land of *if only*. Until today, Bonnie had known, for certain, that Hank would not, could not ever change. His wall of silence, shutting her out, had been the one immutable fact of Bonnie's existence. She'd been free to blame him for her failures, while dreaming of all the great things she'd do if not for his cold, heartless personality. Now, inexplicably, Hank was not here. Whether Hope had duped him into a fool's errand, or lured him with her open admiration—either way, it was uncharacteristic of Hank to go out of his way for anyone. Evidently, Hank was not as set in his ways as Bonnie had believed, and that realization sent her self-righteousness tumbling to the ground.

Her chores completed, Bonnie gazed at a bold sunset, a crisp reddish-orange circle, vanishing inch by inch below the horizon. Hank, she realized, had not been the only one hiding behind a wall of silence. Her own, carefully groomed resentments loomed large. If Hank was capable of change, why had she given up on him years ago, putting all her energy into her writing and none into her marriage? Was it too late, now, to give it another try? She thought about praying but felt unworthy. So, she simply covered her face and uttered, "God help me."

After a long silence, Bonnie raised her head and took a deep breath. She headed down the short lane to the mailbox to gather the mail. Back in the house, she plopped herself back in Hank's chair, mail on her lap. A telephone statement, a gas and electricity bill, a reminder to renew Hank's Sports Illustrated, and a free periodical, "Beginning With Jesus." A bookmark came with it with the inscription, *My grace is sufficient for you, for My power is made perfect in weakness. 1 Corinthians 12:9.*

She read it several times and then said simply, "I'm sorry. I need some help, God." Picking up *Tangled Web* from beside the chair, she leafed through it again, a business card slipping out.

**Hope Hoover Claude**
the *Messenger*
Specialty: human interest stories

Hope's number was on the back side. Was this all a ruse, some nasty trick?

Leaving the mail in the chair, Bonnie stood up, determinedly walked to the kitchen and dialed the number.

Hope....

# NORMA'S CLASS REUNION

With her window facing east, Norma allowed the sun to awaken her each morning. After making the bed and fluffing the pillows in the just-right position against the headboard, she began her stretching exercises. Although boring at times, she understood the benefits of maintaining her strength, flexibility, and increased circulation and stuck to the daily routine. Finished and more alert, she wound the plush, terry-cloth robe around her mature shape and padded quietly to the bathroom. As she washed her face and applied moisturizer, she noted a new crease between her eyebrows. If she knew now what she didn't know so long ago, she would have taken better care of her birthday suit. The label should have read: "Do not bleach, do not tumble dry, handle with care, this is not stain resistant."

Neither did Norma's mother know all that a parent needs to know in raising a child. And so Norma worked as a lifeguard at the municipal pool, walked beans in her bare feet, and de-tasseled corn before sunscreen was a necessity. She drank from a hose attached to the hydrant by the barn, climbed the farm windmill, and devoured ice cream on a nightly basis. She washed her face only when she felt like it and never knew that hydrating was important in all things related to health and beauty. Emotionally pampered by her hard-working mother and told she would amount to much more than a farmer's wife, she grew with a healthy work ethic but with a somewhat self-important attitude. When the evolution between carefree, animated, young girl to petty, egotistical adult occurred, no one knew. It was something Norma never gave a thought to. Why would she? She was Norma Schultz.

Wondering how this newly discovered wrinkle could have happened, Norma considered her reflection and made a mental note to call her hairdresser for another color. The last treatment had not brightened her face the way the stylist had promised. She prodded the crease, tried to relax it and make it less visible while attempting to ignore the crow's feet etched in the corners of her eyes.

In the kitchen she measured out three tablespoons of steel-cut oatmeal into a cereal bowl and set out multi-grain bread and almond butter as the coffee pot finished perking, having been set at this very time to do so. Carrying the coffee to her lace-covered dining room table, she settled the mug on a matching coaster and opened her Bible study to Galatians 5:22. She read aloud:

"But the fruit of the Spirit is joy, peace, patience, kindness, goodness, faithfulness, gentleness and self-control," she recited and took pleasure in the sound of her voice. With the first sip of caffeine coursing through her veins, Norma prayed silently, *Search me O God and know my heart; test me and know my anxious thoughts. See if there is any offensive way in me and lead me in the way everlasting.*

She skipped over the following verses having to do with *living by the Spirit* and *Let us not become conceited, provoking and envying each other….* and closed her Bible. Letting her mind wander a bit, she asked God, what about *the* love, *the* joy, *the* peace?—feeling little of these in her life. She believed she had shown evidence of all the other fruits, especially the self-control. Norma's predictable routine provided comfort, and although some of the fruits were apparently missing in her life, she never worried about her soul— until Tim came back into her life.

⋅⋅◆◆◆◆⋅⋅

Norma never married. She had dates, lots of them as a young girl, and even though this all occurred decades ago, she spent increasingly sleepless nights reflecting on what may have gone wrong in each relationship. She was the Lee County Pork Queen, 1954. If you don't get the significance of this, you did not grow up a farmer's daughter. She went to prom three years in a row with some of the best looking guys in high school. In college, she was engaged for a short period of time. John and she studied together, discussed economics and business law in the wee hours of the morning, and shared an occasional pizza. When John left for law school in another state, and she left for a job opportunity in the state capital as an accountant, the relationship withered and died. Preparing and examining financial accounts and checking the accuracy of records filled her days. Employers touted her efficiency and organizational skills.

Although retired, she didn't think of herself as old; however, she knew that she was headed in that direction with no U-turns, detours, or STOP signs ahead. She had watched her parents grow old, get sick, and die. She understood the invisible walls that surface with aging: can't go there, don't go there, not safe anymore—things she would not be able to do, places she would not be able to go because she would not be what she used to be. And lately she questioned if *what she used to be* was even worthy.

As a young girl, after supper time, she waited until her parents nodded off in front of the black and white television set. While Walter Cronkite broadcast the 10 p.m. news, she left the house and walked the quarter-mile farm lane. Plopping herself in the soft ditch grass and allowing the heavens to saturate her space, she imagined that the world had possibilities just for her, and they were infinite. Now, the slivers of open spaces were narrowing. She rode an exercise bike instead of walking due to arthritis in her feet. She could not eat just anything she wanted; the doctors had diagnosed her with irritable bowel syndrome. The phrase, itself, made her wince. Technology drives the world, but sometimes Norma could not determine how to solve a simple tech glitch. She began to feel inconsequential at a meeting, or a gathering—thinking that she had nothing to offer. Trendy music, movies, and clothing seemed senseless, irrational.

Loneliness at some point creeps into a person's core. Norma surprised even herself one night when she discovered that she had opened her computer to a dating site. Surely, there were others like her out there waiting for someone like her—a nice girl, still attractive, financially stable, and looking for a little adventure. What would it hurt?…. OurTime, eharmony, and more greeted her with success stories from those who took a chance on love. *Willie and I met on-line and talked for weeks before meeting in person. We decided to live together. I've never been happier.* And another, *I have found the love of my life after all of these years.* As she scanned her potential matches, however, she thought that these men came across as different, odd, and, heaven forbid, pretentious. She decided to discuss this with her friend, Carol, her only confidant. Carol was a few years younger than Norma and might be able to offer advice.

-------◆◆◆◆◆◆-------

They met at the local coffee shop, Old Main, on a Saturday morning. The place was busier than usual as the class of '55 was in town for a reunion. Norma ordered regular coffee, no cream and sugar, and Carol requested a low-fat, sugar-free latte. A group of women noisily crowded in the back entrance dressed simply but elegantly from head to toe, in layers, fashionable scarves around their necks, comfortable but classy shoes. Designer purses were attached to their shoulders. Various fragrances surrounded them as they approached the Old Main menu options offering everything from latte, espresso, and tea, to Italian sodas.

"Oooh, they're all looking at us," Carol said, an out-of-towner herself.

"Have you ever noticed how funny old people are?" Norma suggested while critically giving each newcomer a once-over. Carol sighed and patted Norma's aging hand while they watched one of the ladies leave the group and start to their table. She took little steps, gripped the table to balance herself, and leaned close as if to get a better look.

"Do I know you? Are you from here?" she asked Carol.

"No," Carol replied sweetly. "I'm not from here, but Norma here...."

"Nice to meet you, Norma," the lady said and turned back to Carol. "The weather is fantastic. We drove all the way this morning, left around 6 a.m. It'll be a full day but it will be worth it. Seeing so many. Your health, it's okay, right? You look good."

"*My* health?" Carol rolled her eyes and looked sideways at Norma before answering, "It's all good. Thanks for asking. I'm afraid we don't know you. What's your name?"

"Shirley," the lady answered as if they should know. "Shirley Newton, one of five sisters." She inched her face towards Carol, cleared her throat, and shuffled away. Norma noticed that the lady's shoes slipped off the back of her heels when she walked revealing compression hose. Norma had the same exact paisley pattern at home. The back of Shirley's head showed a bald spot, probably from sleeping in the same place for too long.

"Is it any wonder that older people scare young children...." Norma said to Carol and raised her eyebrows, the forehead wrinkles becoming dominant. "The little steps by large people, the eye contact within inches of your face, the complex clothing, the questions. What child has ever asked you about your health or wanted to talk about the weather?"

"Sure, I get what you mean." Carol agreed but wondered if Norma had ever been around a small child in her lifetime. The two watched the colorful cluster move as one towards the exit, a straggler or two bringing up the rear. One or two turned to take one last look at Carol and Norma and give a brief wave.

"Hey, what's this I hear about you wanting to try on-line dating?" Carol asked.

"On-line dating?" Norma asked, immediately frightened. "I'm just looking, you know. I never said anything about *dating*." The term, dating, bothered her. What would the proper word be at her age if she were to have a gentleman caller? "I'm not sure if I'm ready, and besides, the internet is sometimes scary. What do you think?"

"I agree; the internet can be frightening." Carol responded. "The world is constantly changing," Carol continued and tried to determine how to put her friend at ease. "For example, I was checking out the Reader's Digest vocabulary the other day and none of the words could be found in my Webster's New Collegiate Dictionary that I got when I graduated high school."

Norma finished her coffee, looked at her watch, and placed her hands on her lap. She had hoped for encouragement. The fact that Carol's dictionary was no longer practical had nothing to do with her need for a relationship.

"Hey, you know what," Carol said interrupting Norma's thoughts. "Why not get out your yearbook? Probably got a few widowers who need some companionship by this time in their lives. Maybe, there's someone you already know that you could connect with."

Norma thought about Carol's words on her way home. There was the quarterback who she had always wanted to date. News spread that his wife had suddenly passed. She had gone with Jim Stensrud, another football player, to prom her junior year. He became an attorney and had a home in Arizona and a lakeside place on Big Spirit Lake. He had divorced at a young age and never remarried. Perhaps Carol was on to something.

She returned to her one-story, cozy apartment and pulled the yearbook from a box in the storage closet and started to leaf through it. Would she even recognize Jim or the quarterback, whatever his name was…. She found her own senior class picture and was pleased that she had not changed that much. Her hair was still short and curly, although the color changed on a whim. *Nice looking*, she thought. She puffed with pride as she read the lengthy list of the activities she was involved in—a much longer listing than anyone else's. She flipped a few more pages and realized that she didn't remember many of her classmates. There was Eileen Wills who had tried to befriend her. Eileen had five brothers, never dressed very well; they just didn't have that much in common.

A yawn slipped out and then another. Norma placed the yearbook beside her on the couch; the pages fell open to the M's. There was Arthur Mack, Lois Martin, and then a name that sounded familiar: Tim Mills. She studied the picture—dark haired, dark-eyed, looking somewhat devious—and recalled that he was the neighbor boy who lived down the road from their farm. They occasionally played together on summer days; and during the school year, they rode the same bus and often shared a seat. Tim never said much of anything to her, but they'd knock each others' shoes together on the ride home. That was about it. Awkward boy, never fit in much with the others, and by the time high school started, she didn't even remember him being around.

"Hmmm," Norma said aloud. "I'm surprised he graduated." *Not likely to be at the reunion*, she thought.

Instead of her usual nap, Norma thought back on her life and what she had accomplished. She made a mental list of topics she could talk about at the coming evening's event. Other classmates might be interested in her past career as an accountant, her trips to England, the notables she had met during her travels. She needed to be prepared and just maybe, just maybe, there may be someone attending who might be interested in some kind of relationship. Someone to go out to dinner with, maybe a movie. Even a phone conversation would be nice.

A new pantsuit with matching scarf and sensible shoes were laid out in the extra bedroom. She allowed extra time to dress; compression hose were sometimes difficult to get on. Sprinkling rose talcum powder in both shoes and a little down her neckline, she wrapped the scarf around her neck. She had checked the menu earlier to make sure nothing would be served that would disagree with her tender digestive system. Chicken and rice with almonds, a garden salad, wheat rolls, and various cheesecakes sounded safe.

She arrived early to the Class of '55 reception and watched from her car while others parked and walked in. She didn't recognize anyone. It had been over 60 years, and she had not bothered to attend any of the previous reunions. A few arrived with canes and walkers. The handicapped parking spaces were full. Norma took a deep breath, grabbed her hefty purse, and got out of the car as gracefully as she could. Leaning on the hood of her vehicle, she stepped up the curb, and started up the sidewalk questioning her decision to come with every step she took. Someone startled her at the door.

"Welcome. So glad you came." A woman greeted her with a handshake. Her name tag read, Susan Armstrong. Norma didn't recognize her. Another stood at a table with name tags.

"Can I help you?" It was the lady from Old Main who had interrupted this morning's coffee with her friend, Carol. Norma peered at the name tag: Shirley Newton.

"Ah, yes I'm Norma Schultz. Is this the class of 1955 reunion?"

"Of course. You're in the right spot. Didn't I see you this morning?"

Someone tapped her on the shoulder. Norma looked at the name on the tag: Raymond Smith. The quarter back? He had a cane and a younger woman at his side. The room crowded, chatter abounded, and Norma grew anxious. She was relieved when everyone was directed to the dining area. She found her name on a place card and was glad to take a seat. As she hung her purse on the back of the chair and removed her brand new scarf which now felt itchy and hot, a gentleman rolled up in his electric wheel chair and sat at the end of the table, adjacent to her.

"Hi," he said and looked at her name tag. "My goodness, Norma Schultz? You're kidding me. I haven't heard a thing about you for decades." Norma, round eyed, was momentarily speechless.

"I'm sorry, but I can't place you," she finally said.

"We were neighbors; we rode the bus together. Tim Mills!" He pointed at his name tag with a shortened pointer finger and then flapped the place card with his name on it in front of her face.

"Of course," she said, embarrassed by his excessive mannerisms. Hoping to quiet him, she added, "I'm sorry I didn't recognize you." He was mostly bald; a few wisps of grey hair were combed over his ears. She recalled the yearbook picture of a dark-eyed, dark haired young man and without thinking commented, "You've changed so much."

He chuckled, shook his head, and tapped his forefingers on the table. She noticed that parts of his fingers were missing. Norma was puzzled. This was Tim, her neighbor, the kid she used to play with during summer months? What happened to the somewhat quiet, but devious little boy? And what happened to his fingertips?

"You never knew did you?" he asked noting that she was eyeing his deformed hands.

"I'm sorry, but I don't know what you referring to," Norma replied, uncomfortable with the conversation.

"We played together as little kids—once in a while, that is; shared a bus seat. In high school, I was a trouble-maker, a risk-taker. You were out of my league, you know, smart, off to college. I had a big crush on you, but we weren't little kids any more. By that time, I sat at the back of the bus; you sat in the front."

He kept drumming his fingertips on the table; Norma could not stop paying attention to them. She looked around the room for another place to sit. She felt a hot flash coming on and knew that she had taken every layer off that she possibly could. Norma fanned herself with her napkin. Tim seemed not to notice her discomfort.

He raised his hands and tapped his finger stubs together. "Yeah, these hands. Froze my fingertips off. I was drinking one night at a friend's, tried to get home. It was winter. Brutally cold. Car stalled out. No gloves in the car. Got out, started to walk home. Saw your yard light but walked right past. Didn't want to bother you…. Farther than I thought." Tim stopped and looked out a nearby window. Norma's heart missed several beats. An ache overwhelmed her chest.

"I'm sorry, so sorry," Norma said. "I had no idea." She was relieved when the salads were served.

"Oh, it was my fault," Tim said and stuffed a napkin inside his collar. "I don't know why I even brought it up. Guess I thought you might have heard about it. You know, small-town news gets around." Norma had a hard time swallowing the lettuce. The dressing made her choke.

"Excuse me," she said to Tim and headed to the restroom. She entered a stall and stood there for as long as she dared. She considered leaving, going home, and wondered why she thought she should come. *For this?* Here, at this place, this reunion, she thought she might have an opportunity for some kind of connection, finally, before it all ended before there was no more. She used the restroom, washed her hands, and patted her face with a wet paper towel noting that the new wrinkle on her forehead was deeper than ever. She returned to the place at the table and wished that she was in her cozy house watching the public television network.

"You okay?" Tim asked. "I'm sorry if I offended you in any way."

"Of course, I'm okay, and I apologize for my poor table manners; I'm just a little off tonight," Norma said and passed on the cheesecake.

A short program started with a few sharing memoires. Norma was not a part of any of them. When everyone started to leave, Tim tapped her on the shoulder. "Here, this is my business card. Give me a call if you like. We could check out the old neighborhood. My son still lives on the home place."

"Ah, thank you," Norma replied. And remembering her manners, added, "I'm glad you came."

"Me, too," Tim answered, his dark eyes twinkled, and he offered his hand. Norma felt his strong grip wrap around her fingers.

When home, she took a hot shower, sleeping medication, and climbed into bed feeling purposeless, unwanted, unloved. She also remembered Tim's handshake—warm and reassuring in some small way. Unable to sleep, she got out of bed, and put the tea kettle on the stove. As she waited for the steam to rise, she retrieved his business card from the bottom of her purse.

---

**Tim Mills**

Regional Operations Manager
World Vision
*Let my heart be broken with the
things that break God's heart.*
Bob Pierce, World Vision founder

---

With a cup of herbal tea in her hands, she thought about her life and determined she had become a bit of a zombie—her mindless thoughts on vanity, her career, her meticulousness with routine. What exactly would it look like, feel like to become more adventurous, to be heedless of others' opinions, to have her soul ignited by something bigger than Norma Schultz? Starting to doze, she climbed into bed and tried to imagine the possibilities.

On Sunday, she brewed a pot of coffee, eliminated breakfast and lunch, and stayed in her soft, cushy robe all day. Sitting at her dining room table and watching the slivers of sunlight dance between the clouds, her morning prayer came to mind, *Lord, test me and know my anxious thoughts. See if there is any offensive way in me and lead me in the way everlasting.* She felt her chest ache and noticed that her heart beat seemed fast and irregular. She picked up her cell phone and considered dialing 911. Her eyes drifted back to the clouds; she breathed deeply; she thought about her childhood and remembered plopping herself in the farm ditch, looking at the stars, and feeling she had the whole world at her fingertips. A smile tugged at the corners of her lips.

At 5 p.m., she opened a can of soup and let the tears stream as it warmed on the stove. At 6 p.m., she picked up Tim's business card and punched in the numbers of his cell phone printed on the backside. He answered on the third ring.

"Tim? Norma Schultz. If you're still in town on Monday, could we meet for lunch?"

*Time is the most precious gift because you only have a set amount of it. You can make more money, but you can't make more time. When you give someone your time, you are giving them a portion of your life that you'll never get back. Your time is your life.*

Rick Warren

# Once Upon a Time

"Once upon a time, a baby girl arrived in a bundle at our house," my mother would say. It didn't matter who was listening. In the grocery aisle to a fellow shopper, a comment to the waitress at The Maidrite, or picking up a conversation with our neighbors over the backyard fence. It was her way of drawing attention to me, their precious daughter. The words would change as the years passed. "Once upon a time, Mandy had a grand birthday party and no one could remove the smile from her face." I remember leaving for the University of Iowa my freshman year, unloading my possessions at the Mayflower, my parents saying goodbye from the dorm parking lot, and my mother whispering in my ear, "Once upon a time, my little girl went off to college..." I felt her warm tears trickle down my neck as Dad took in the scene, his buttons ready to pop.

Four years later, I was hired as a high school English teacher in the small town of Solon, about ten miles from Iowa City. My parents visited my classroom before the school year started. Mom roamed about taking in the bulletin boards, the bookshelves. She fingered the items on my desk, the stapler, a container for pencils and pens, a gradebook with pupils' names already printed neatly inside. She walked to the September, 1974, calendar posted on a bulletin board and flipped backwards to August and then July and took a deep breath.

"I can't believe this," she said. "Where does the time go?"

"Yes, Momma, once upon a time," I said, "your little girl grew up and became a teacher." She looked longingly at me as if she didn't want to let go.

As the months, a year and more passed in this small rural community, I became quite familiar with students, their families, and their circumstances and felt that I had made a new home. A school year has its highlights:

homecoming, Halloween, Thanksgiving, Christmas, the New Year, a second semester, Valentine's Day, prom, and graduation. With each new season or event, bulletin boards were switched, along with topics to be covered in a particular subject area. I even had my teacher clothes. A sweater with orange pumpkins and falling leaves, a sweatshirt with basketball players listed on the back with the date of their last tournament run, a jumper with a Valentine's heart on a pocket. There were always occasions to turn over a new leaf, begin anew with little celebrations and new starts.

I felt comfortable living in the upstairs of an older renovated house where the owner, Mrs. Bisbee, a widow, lived below me. She shared her growing up stories, some history of the area, and her homemade raisin oatmeal cookies. She also asked questions—some, which I preferred not to answer.

"You're so pretty, so competent. You surely have someone special in your life?" She inquired.

"Not really. I haven't had time," I explained. "I love teaching; it's enough for me."

"*Really*, Mandy? A nice girl like you needs a good man in her life. Companionship is a wonderful thing." With this, she would venture off into a time her husband, Willard, and she traveled the country in their reliable Chevy, a map on her lap, pointing out landscapes, and visitor centers. She shared their interest in gardening and the growing-up stories of their precious son, Will.

She delighted in hearing about my teaching experiences, and I was willing to tell her about how my day had gone at school and what assignments were given. She was especially intrigued by my Creative Writing class, an upper level high school course. At the beginning of one year, I gave the writing task titled, *Once Upon a Time*. Thinking of my mother's musings, but realizing some students would venture into the fairy tale genre, I looked forward to what it might prompt. A few squirmed in their seats. James, the intellectual analyzer, looked at his watch. Sidney chewed on her erasure. Others whispered; a few opened their notebooks.

"Miss Herman?" Roj, a student with periodic episodes of ADHD, wildly waved his hand back and forth. "Could you be more specific?" The class moaned.

"Well, Roj," I replied, "this is a creative writing class, so let your imagination take wings and see what you can come up with." A buzzer singled the end of a class period as I regretted the use of my own cliché—*let your imagination take wings*. As the classroom emptied, various comments lingered.

"I'm gonna write about growing up in California," Carmen announced. "We spent a lot of time at the beach."

"Boring," our star basketball center mumbled.

Leonard, my shy, freckled loner, approached my desk, "I've always wanted to write about space, you know, in a fantasy fiction way." I gave him a thumbs-up and nodded my head. "You mean, that's okay?" he asked.

"Of course, Leonard," I replied. "I'm looking forward to reading what you come up with."

I assumed that most of the assignments would be take-offs from fairy tales or mini autobiographies. A week later when narratives were handed in, I was surprised and impressed with one girl's rendition.

Creative Writing Assignment for Miss Herman
Submitted by Sidney Peterson

**Once upon a time, I lived in a bubble**. I faced whatever life handed me with confidence—due to a strong family support system and a dose of naivety. I thought my version of the world was everyone else's. I have discovered that friends and loved ones who I thought were as "secure" as I was were not. Some had elephants in the living room, on the back steps, and out on their lawns. I became aware that shame is not shared. It's there; it exists; but, it is not talked about.

Recently, I have tried to understand the bigger picture of relationship issues—including abuse, poverty, and mental illness—especially after reading two books by Dave Pelzer (*A Child Called 'It'* and *A Man Named Dave*) for my reading class. I thought about a friend or two and family members who hid things. Certain concerns were never discussed out in the open but in whispers behind closed doors or in muffled discussions deep in the night. I didn't know whether to satisfy my curiosity or to pretend I was unaware of any of it.

I read somewhere that everyone we meet in life, every experience we have, shape us into the person we become. This has to include those who have been loving to us; but also has to include those who have not been loving. It could include others who one may meet for short periods of his or her life. Those who leave loving imprints; those who leave harmful imprints. All leave forever marks.

Maybe, what I didn't "get" before, I have a chance to get now. I mentioned this to my best friend when we were talking about life and how it is not fair for some. I told her that I felt a need to make a difference — although I wasn't sure what I even meant or how to go about it.

I don't know how to go forward with all this. I just know that because I am aware of so-called "hidden issues," I feel that I may have a responsibility to do something about it. That scares me.

---

It scared me, too; I wondered what her experiences were that caused such wisdom and insight at age sixteen. It bothered me that she felt a sense of responsibility for something that seemed out of her control. Later in the week, I asked Sidney, the pencil chewer, to meet me after school to discuss her assignment. She was careful with her words.

"This is confidential, Miss Herman. I wrote it in a few minutes. I know you were thinking fairy tales, but this…. It just came out. It's like I couldn't help it."

"No, I appreciate what you have written. It shows wisdom and understanding beyond your years." A slight smile tugged at her upper lip but immediately disappeared. The phrases, *my version of the world, elephants in the living room, relationship issues,* were curious statements from someone like Sidney who seemed to portray the All-American girl with her clear complexion, a sense of strength in her demeanor, and her quiet confidence.

"Please, don't let anyone else read it," she requested and brought her hands to her face.

"Of course," I replied and paused. "Can I ask you a few questions?" Sidney's eyes darted to the closed classroom door, scanned the empty seats of the classroom, and shrugged.

"Are *you* okay?" I had to know. As a teacher I was a mandatory reporter for abuse. It was a part of my job.

"Yes, I'm fine." She shrugged her shoulders again. "I guess it's okay to tell you. It's my aunt. You wouldn't know her."

I was confused. "You're concerned about your aunt?"

"… I guess so. I mean things have happened, and we can't do anything about it." Her eyes started to tear. I didn't want to make her cry. I decided not to press further. There was no need; Sidney opened up.

"She has this kid. Well, Jack's not a kid anymore. My cousin. He's been in a lot of trouble. My aunt tries to make everything better by covering up stuff. But, it's impossible. My uncle is mean and it's like he expects his kid to be that way, too. They all live in a run-down house in the middle of no-where. Mom doesn't know how to help her without involving our family in their family problems. She's even afraid for our safety if we do. That's how bad it is."

I felt a chill, stood up, and went to the window to close it. The name *Jack* disturbed me. How many Jacks were there who had mean dads, who lived in a run-down house in the middle of nowhere….

"Your cousin? His name is *Jack*?" I took a deep breath, needing more information. "You mentioned that he'd been in a lot of trouble. What kind of trouble, Sidney?"

"Yeah. He's not able to keep a job, still lives at home, kind of a loner but hangs out at the bars in Iowa City, where the university is. You know the one you went to." Memories like quick movie clips flicked through my mind; the pit of my stomach stirred. "He's even been in jail, but I can't remember what he did."

"Where does your aunt live?"

"It's a little town. Mom calls it Down-in-the-Boondocks." Sidney laughed; a nervous cough escaped. "It's about twenty miles from here. We never go there anymore. It's too sad. It's my mom's sister, and we can't do anything about it. She used to be my favorite aunt; it all sort of fell apart."

"This family, they live in town?" I continued to pry.

"Oh, sorry, no. It's outside town, an acreage. Acreage is kind of a fancy word though. It's rundown, old. Once some state officials came out because a neighbor turned my uncle in because of the health of their animals, all sickly and under-fed, I guess...."

I stopped listening, hearing only Sidney's bits and pieces—a family argument, Jack's bullying, his dad explaining it as "boy behavior." My own jumbled memories surfaced. The animals' sounds—a bellow, a grunt, the rustling of hooves— inside the barn that night. I went to the window, again, opening it. Perspiration prickled my armpits and temples; heat crept up my neck and a mixture of guilt, shame, and confusion trickled through my veins.

"Are you okay, Miss Herman?" Sidney asked. "We can do this another time."

"Sidney, did Jack or anyone in his family ever harm you?"

"Oh, no. Of course not. I was just a kid then... Are you all right?"

"I'm sorry. It's the end of the day, and I guess I'm a little worn out," I lied and turned the focus back on Sidney. "Why did you write this? Is it because you want to help your aunt?"

"It just came out. Like I said, don't share it with anyone. I'm kinda' sorry I wrote it. Do you want me to write something else? I could do that...." She looked at the large white-faced clock above my desk. 5:00. "I gotta go," she said, pulled her backpack off the floor, and started to leave. "You won't tell anyone, right? My mom and dad would really be upset."

"Of course not," I replied, and understood that if I had done something years ago, this young girl's heart would be in a happier place, and Sidney's aunt might be in a better place, a protected place, a safe place, a place where she could have found happiness. And Jack? I pushed it from my mind as I had been doing for years.

That evening, I opened a can of tomato soup. As it heated on the small apartment stove, I slapped together two slices of whole wheat bread with two slices of cheese in the middle and stuck it in the oven. Waiting for it to get crispy-chewy, I walked to the picture window in my living room. Troubling clouds loomed. A grumble shuttled from horizon to horizon, lightning skittled across the heavens, and as each raindrop splashed on the glass, an image appeared. I could not stop them: a girl plummeting into a ditch, unending rows of corn, a shanty of a farmhouse, a man with bulging lips, a lady running in a flimsy housedress.

I shook the fading imageries from my head and returned to the stove where the soup simmered. Sidney's "Once Upon a Time" angered me. It was not her fault; it was mine. I had chosen to hide the memory, even bury it. In fact, pretending none of it had happened probably kept me from developing any kind of intimate relationship, the kind of relationship Mrs. Bisbee thought I was worthy of. And, here, this young woman, Sidney, with her *Once Upon a Time* assignment brought everything tumbling back.

The following day, I pulled a map from my glove compartment and took it up to my apartment. The little town of Downsey, Sidney's "Down-in-the-Boondocks," was only a half hour away, yet it seemed like another life time, another country. It was a journey that should have been taken long ago.

On Saturday morning, I threw a few things in the car—Diet Pepsi, a jacket, the map. Back in the house, I filled a bowl with cold cereal and milk and swallowed it, not tasting a bite. I filled the car with gas, checked the map again, and headed out of town with no particular plan. Crossing a bridge and noting the creek run below, I thought of Heraclitus' words. He was a pre-Socratic Greek philosopher who thought of himself as a pioneer of wisdom. As I remembered, "You cannot step twice in the same river," I thought of the wispy cotton seeds in the air that ended up floating the river, bubbles at various spots, sticks here and there, the current, the sun's reflections at various times of the day, a rock tossed... and understood how nothing ever stays the same. Nothing. As the miles passed, I thought of my parents who loved me unconditionally. Mom and Dad were hard-working farmers who worked the land, raised a menagerie of cattle, pigs, and chickens to keep food on the table and clothes on our backs. A horse that enjoyed having his muzzle tickled, enough cats to keep the mice away from the barn, and a Border Collie were part of our extended family.

I pictured my parents watching Lawrence Welk. They each had separate agendas during the day, but when Lawrence Welk came on, they were in the living room together. Mom would be humming while she rocked in her favorite chair, and Dad would be perusing the newspaper with a glimpse of the television now and then. I wanted to be home with them in my pajamas with a bowl of popcorn on my lap waiting for the Lennon Sisters.

"You can't really be interested in this," my mother might say.

"*You* like Lawrence Welk. What's wrong with him?" I would answer. She would laugh, wink at me, and add, "Better pop some more popcorn. Your dad might like some."

Their ordinary life had provided me security. Would I ever have what my parents had? A loving, life-time relationship; companionship; children? How could I have let one night's events with a guy named Jack take my life on a course I would never have chosen? Had it even been a conscious choice? I had capsulized it, repressed it, and pretended none of it had happened. It had worked until Sidney's own "Once Upon a Time" ended up on my desk.

I reached Downsey, drove over the railroad tracks and past the grain bins. That night that I accepted a ride home from a stranger named Jack had been dark and rainy, so the surroundings were not familiar. However, after a few turns, I recognized his parents' place. The sun was bright. The fields were sprouting with shoots of beans and corn, but the farmstead was still in shambles, the grove thickness hovering above like blobs of dark green ink. A single emaciated cow leaned against the barn door, a few chickens scattered as I drove past, made a u-turn at the intersection, and drove by again. No Firebird; no rusted out truck. But, there she was, bent over a scraggly hodgepodge of wild flowers, her hair covering her face—the lady in the flimsy dress. Sidney's aunt? I turned in and stopped a few feet from her flower patch. She pulled the weeds one by one with her right hand and clutched the pulled ones with her left.

"Hi," I called. She rose slowly and placed the fist, full of weeds, on her back, turned, and studied me.

"Hi," I repeated and tried a smile. She looked towards the house and then the barn.

"It's just me; no one's here," she said.

I took a couple of steps closer. "Do you remember me?" I asked cautiously.

She nodded her head slowly. "Maybe."

"I came to thank you. For what you did. It's been a while… Jack? Is he your son? I was with him one night. We ended up here. You gave me some keys so I could get home." It was a vague and decent version of what had happened, but I didn't know how else to tell it.

"Jack. Yes, I guess you could call him my son although it hurts to do so." She studied the treetops beginning to twist with the wind and then carried her fistful of weeds to a pile at the corner of her flower patch and dropped them. "Step-son. Caused a lot of pain over the years. Still lives here when he's around. Hasn't been for a while." She wiped her hands on a wrinkled and stained apron. "Sorry, but I don't know your name."

I heard an engine growling, coughing, and sputtering in the distance and pictured the rusted out truck.

"Your husband?" I asked.

"Probably better leave," she said and waved me away from her.

"Can I come again?" I asked. She coughed and hacked up phlegm. It dribbled down her chin, a pinkish goo. She wiped it away with her apron bottom. "Are you sick?" I questioned.

Ignoring my question, she tromped towards the house, stepping clumsily on her newly weeded wildflowers, hacking with each step. Getting in my car, I put on my sunglasses and a billed cap and turned the key. The diesel truck pulled up beside me, blocking my exit.

"Whatcha' want, girlie?" The word girlie disgusted me as much as it had several years ago.

"Just trying to get directions," I fibbed. "Took the wrong turn."

"You ain't got no business here girlie. Best be on your way." A cigar hung from his protruding lips. I placed the car in reverse to get around him and then raced down the road, heart throbbing.

Eyes on the road in front of me, I headed back to Downsey while a narrative inside my head appeared in neatly typed paragraphs. I pulled off on a field drive to concentrate on them.

*A white dog with brown spots, his nose wet and cold, growled. Cowering on her scraped knees on a brittle cement walk, a little girl covered her face with her hands and wished him away. Her doll lay scattered in pieces before her. Footsteps approached. Someone tapped her shoulder. "You all right, honey? The dog, he's gone. Mean ol' thing. Has nothin' to do all day 'cept scare little ones like you." A lady took her hankie, wiped the little one's tears and then her knees. "You run along home now. Your Gramma be lookin' for you."*

Strange, I thought. I was probably five years old and staying at Grandma's house. I never told my Grandmother because I didn't want to get into trouble. I had gone into a neighborhood she had forbidden. A few weeks later, there was a front page article in our small town newspaper about another little girl getting bitten by this same dog. Stitches covered her face; the owner was charged. I did not eat supper that night. My thoughts were filled with something I had failed to do.

Another story appeared, again in neatly typed paragraphs.

*"What's up?" Ann asked. Two girls, heads together, hands heavy with textbooks and notebooks, on their way to World History. Semester test day. They both look at the overhead clock.*

*"We're goin' be late," Mandy says. Always the goodie-two-shoes, a bit of a worrier, an over-achiever.*

*"Hey, wait up," Ann says. "I need a favor."*

*"Not now," Mandy replies.*

*"Yeah, now, really!" Ann persists. "I forgot to study. Let's sit together. You'll help me out, right?"*

That was high school. So, I wasn't perfect, I thought. Ann went on to college but dropped out unable to cope with the rigor in an academic world. And, here I was on a journey of sorts to clear my conscience of something that happened in college and this mumble-jumble from my childhood turns up. It frustrated me. And then another typewritten page, this one in bold: IT'S NOT JUST ABOUT YOU.

I put the car back in gear and continued to Downsey, passed a smattering of worn out houses, and noted a small rectangular building with a U.S. Postal Service sign posted on a weathered door. I parked and got out of the car. A dog barked from a far. I heard a door slam down the street. Inside the building, an elderly man with an apron and postal cap stood at the counter with a shocked look. Probably hadn't had a customer in weeks.

"Gotta a sheriff in town or police officer?" I asked.

"Somethin' wrong?" he asked, his eyebrows wiggled.

"No, I need to report something," I said. He left me, limped to the back room and came back with a card. The sheriff's office number was listed.

"Use that. We don' see cops or the like around here. Don' have any problems either. Quiet community. Just the way we like it." He eye-balled me suspiciously until I felt like a trouble-maker.

I left the post office, passed over the railroad tracks, sped by the humongous grain bins still full with last fall's bounty, and started the curved highway that would take me out of town when a large church loomed ahead, its steeple with cross pointed toward the heavens. It was off the highway a ways and surrounded by a field of oats and a few curious sunflowers. I pulled into its empty graveled parking lot. I hadn't been to a church in years in spite of my parents' encouragement. Taking the steps to the front oak doors, I tugged until it opened, and stepped inside. A banner hung to my left. Someone with beautiful calligraphy had written, *In the same way, even though we are many individuals, Christ makes us one body and individuals who are connected to each other. Romans 12:5*

A rack of periodicals included copies of "Portals of Prayer" and a stack of the up-coming Sunday bulletins. I picked one up and studied the cover illustration, a copy of Michelangelo's painting, *The Creation of Adam*, depicting God giving life to the first human. Inside the bulletin were announcements about a youth league meeting, a family potluck, Bible study times. The order of the service completed another page with hymn numbers listed. I looked under "Sermon" to see Pastor Warren's name and the title: **Once Upon a Time**. I closed my eyes and looked again, thinking *this is not possible*. But there it was, **Once Upon a Time**. Feeling slightly spooked, I turned to the door leading to the sanctuary and peeked in. Rows and rows of wooden pews faced the pulpit, the communion rail, the cross. It was all so familiar and yet so new. My parents had always taken me to church. I stopped attending in college for no particular reason. Lazy? No longer interested? A wave of longing for a connection to something greater than me, greater than my troubling past, washed through me, and I felt empty and yet open to possibilities. Timidly, I took a few steps on the carpeted aisle, sat in the back pew, my face turned to the cross, and made a choice to remember that night.

1968

The moon deposited dainty slivers on the black, black soil. Hunkered between corn rows, I tried to concentrate on them. Each fluctuated to the shift of the wind or a passing cloud. Shivers covered my arms and legs and trickled down my spine until I could not separate cold from panic. In my mind I tried to determine how I had gotten here.

Thunder rumbled; the light slivers disappeared; a murky darkness settled in. A rustling of leaves caught my attention several rows away. A field animal? Or was it him? Carefully, I flattened myself and became a part of the damp earth. As gloomy as it was and with my dark slacks and black hooded sweater, I prayed he would not see me. The earth smelled fresh, and I wondered if my hammering heart disrupted the life of the beetles, crickets, and various crawling creatures below me.

Someone, out of breath, was near. He separated the stalks and walked through, one of his footsteps within inches of the top of my head.

"Stupid woman," he mumbled. The word *stupid* needled my brain.

He screamed the sound of a wounded animal and ran in the opposite direction of my hideaway, thrashing the stalks, throwing a tantrum like a fuming child. I pictured him with plaid flannel shirt, weathered jeans, work boots with steel toes, stocking cap down to his eyebrows, and my stomach churned. The hot wings I had devoured an hour or so ago burbled up my throat as the Pontiac Firebird squealed away. Again, thunder rumbled; lightning sparked the sky; and rain battered the field. I stood, wrapped my arms around me for warmth, and headed back the direction I had come. Having grown up on a farm, I knew about cornfields and how to get out of one. I also remember seeing a farm light.

I started the trek to the end of the row. With each step, I thought of my parents and how hard they had tried to protect me. But, here I was in some stranger's cornfield because of decisions I had made. I hoped that they were praying for me tonight, at this moment, as they so often told me they did.

I climbed the barbed wire fence at the end of the corn row and spotted the place I had rolled into the ditch after jumping from the Firebird. I thanked God that I only had abrasions and bruises. Standing on the gravel road, I surveyed my surroundings. It continued to rain; however, light travels long distances, and I spotted a car circling the four mile section of land. It had to be him. I had a deep longing to be in my own room, under flannel sheets, my parent's voices seeping up through the floor vent.

Walking through the ditch to keep a low profile, I headed in the direction of the farm light. As the rain dripped down my chin and sloshed inside my shoes, I asked God for forgiveness. After all, it was my decision to accept a ride home from a total stranger, a guy who bought me hot wings and could carry on a reasonable conversation, a guy who wasn't bad looking in spite of the fact that he needed a shower.

"Wanna a ride home?" he had asked.

"I came with friends," I answered.

"So, I can still give you a ride home. Your friends won't care," he said.

Bored, wanting adventure, *was I that lonely?* I accepted. My friends questioned my decision with *are you sure? Do you know him?* I offered *a he's okay, no big deal, headed my way* phrases. Truth be told, it was more than boredom, more than lonely. Desperation would be a better word. I had never been the most popular girl in my class, or on a varsity athletic team, or in the marching band. I was a good student, and my name could be found on the honor roll. But who looks?

I recalled a conversation in science class when choosing groups for a project. I twiddled my pencil and checked the weather outside while others gathered in their cliques. Someone tapped me on the shoulder.

"You, what's your name? You can be in ours," he said. I blushed. He was an athlete and out of my league. I knew I was being asked because of my brains. Can anyone blame me for not feeling confident about myself when it came to the other sex? I thought college would provide opportunities for someone like me. There had to be average-looking guys out there looking for average-looking, nice girls. Here I was in my sophomore year without having been asked out once. So, when this guy sided up to me and asked me, *me*, if he could buy me a drink, of course, I said, yes. One drink led to another. He was easy to talk to and concentrated on my eyes as if he wanted to get to know me.

"Come on, let me give you a ride home," he pleaded.

"You haven't even asked my name." I said with a smile, feeling coy and yet confident.

"I'm Jack, and you're _____?"

"Mandy."

"I like that, Mandy. Good name. Ready?"

"I'm with friends," I said. I looked around the bar and spotted them—both on the dance floor with a partner, the Four Tops hit, "I Can't Help Myself," reverberating from a jukebox.

"We could dance." I suggested. He shook his head.

"They're not going to miss you," he whispered close to my ear. "I would." His breath was moist, warm, and smelled of beer—too much of it. He squeezed my shoulder with one hand and drummed his knuckles on the bar with the other. His hands were rugged. Construction worker?

"What do you do?" I asked.

"Independent contractor," he replied and puffed out his chest. He took one of his hands and placed it on my back. It was warm and strong. Something unfamiliar stirred my core.

"Hey, we can stay here, or we can get to know each other better. Too crowded here. Let's go." Jack cupped my elbow in his palm, stood us both up at the same time, and we walked towards the backdoor of Rusty's. A bouncer stopped us. He was big, broad shouldered. Sweat slid down his sideburns.

"You okay?" the security officer asked and looked directly at me.

"Sure," I answered and pushed Jack's hand away from my elbow.

"Where you headed?" the bouncer continued and looked from Jack to me and back at Jack.

Jack mumbled an expletive and blurted sarcastically, "You work for the FBI or just stickin' your nose in everybody's business?"

"Just doin' my job the best I know how," the bouncer replied. He then looked squarely at me and said, "You take care, Miss."

Discernment, a word my dad often used, was lacking. Rain drops plopped on the windshield of Jack's Firebird; the car's wipers smeared bug goo, greenish yellow, until visibility was limited. Jack stepped on the gas; another driver's horn blew long and hard. I turned around to see a man, one hand on the wheel, the other with a middle finger raised in defiance.

"That was close," I said. "If you've had too much to drink, just let me off. I can walk."

"Shoulda' watched where he was going," Jack replied and snorted.

"Do you know how to get to my dorm, the Mayflower?" I asked.

"Too early for that," he answered.

"Where are we going?" I asked as we turned onto the main highway.

"You ask way too many questions," he chuckled. "Said I'd get you home, and I will. Sit tight."

I watched the white line that divided the highway; I counted the cars going the other direction. Jack was traveling over 80 miles an hour.

"Padiddle!" He yelled and slapped my knee as a car traveled past us with one light out.

"Padiddle?" I questioned.

"Don't know much, do ya?" He pulled me close with his right arm and planted a slobbering kiss on the side of my face. I could not even look at him. Within minutes, he had turned into a disgusting monster. A sign emerged in the fog, Downsey, established 1853, and Jack slowed down.

"Don't want to get picked up, do we?" He chuckled. "You're shy aren't you?" We crossed a railroad track and passed towering grain bins.

"Where's the rest of the town?" I asked.

"This is it," Jack said. "Wanna check out those grain bins? Probably haven't checked them out at night, have you?"

"I've never been here, and I'm not interested in checking out the grain bins."

"Like the car?" He asked, patted the dashboard, and placed his hand on my thigh.

"What year is it?" I tried to keep the conversation ordinary.

He squeezed my inner thigh until it hurt and moved his hand slowly upward. Feeling nauseous, I gripped his thick wrist and dug my fingernails into his skin. He pulled off on a gravel road, spewing gravel.

"What you got on under that sweat shirt?" he asked. I fell silent, my one hand battling the one he had on my leg, the other hand on the passenger-side door handle. My eyes scanned the ditches and passing fields.

"You need to take me home!" I demanded.

"Can't help myself," Jack sneered. "Just like the song. You heard it, baby. Can't help myself."

"Take me home!"

Jack looked at me as if I had spit in his face and stomped on the brakes. The car spun out of control. I tugged on the door handle, pushed the door open, and jumped.

Now, as I continued my trek to the farm light, I asked myself, *What is the worst thing that can happen here? Maybe, Jack's trying to find me and offer an apology.* Considering the turn on an abandoned road, a hand up my shirt and the fiddling with his own worn jeans, I felt shame over my own naivety. Words like *raped, beaten, left-for-dead*, crossed my mind. With one eye on the farm light and one light on the Pontiac Firebird headlights still circling the section, I took one squishy step after another.

The farm light spotted from the cornfield, now hovered above a hefty, sinking barn. A faint rustling came from within—farm animals at rest in their stalls—safe, sound and warm. A rusted out truck sat in the driveway. The house was a fourth of the barn size and needed a coat of paint; a shutter loosed from its moorings hung helter-skelter. Flickers of television bounced from a window and across the wet grass. I considered how to approach this house without frightening anyone, but the Pontiac headlights were still out there, and I needed help and soon. Leaving muddy footprints on the front porch, I knocked gently on the front door. Then, louder. Then, banged my fist. A middle-aged guy in overalls showed his face through the front window. A cigar hung from his bulging lips. Steely eyes measured me from top to bottom.

"I need help," I shouted. Behind me, the Pontiac Firebird pulled into the driveway.

"Please, I need help," I yelled, enunciating each word.

I heard the deadlock bolt slide back. The cigar stayed in his mouth. "What kinda help you need, girlie?" He looked strangely familiar and a mixture of fatigue, regret, and humiliation washed through me.

"Do you have a phone?" I tried.

"No phone, here. Don' need it."

A woman peeked around his bulk, a stooped woman with sad eyes and a worn face.

"What she want?" she asked.

"Nothin', no matter to you. Best git to bed, Mamma."

She took a half a step back and stayed.

With the word *Mamma*, a prayer came to mind. A prayer my own mother often said to herself in times of trial. *God be in my head and in my understanding; God be in my eyes and in my looking...* I searched this woman's worn-out face. Faded-out blue eyes matched the small-flowered print in her cotton house dress. Wispy grey hair surrounded her face.

"No business of yours," her husband whined and prodded her away.

Jack, behind me now, walked up the steps to the porch and stood behind me, hands in his pocket. Waiting.

"I need a ride into town," I explained to the man behind the door. "Can you give me a ride into town?"

"What is it, Dad? What's she want?" Jack asked.

"Phone. Girlie, here, wants a phone. Out in the middle of no where. Can you believe that, Son?" He chuckled, amused. "And, if not a phone, a ride. Can't believe that one either. Must think money grows on trees. A phone, gas for a car. Hey, just thought of somethin'. Son, here, has a car, nice one at that. He'll give you a lift, Girlie."

The door closed; the deadbolt lock clicked into place; the television went dark. This man in overalls, his lips sucking a cigar, watched from the window. As I turned away from the house, Jack gripped my elbow and steered me to the Firebird. *God be in my head and in my understanding; God be in my eyes and in my looking....* and I saw her in my peripheral vision. A figure in white cotton drifting off into the bushes and brambles surrounding the house.

Jack pushed me into the backseat of the car and fastened my seatbelt. He reeked of sweat, beer, and dirt. I heard my mother's words *once upon a time....* and felt a huge sense of regret. How could I ever tell her?

"I'll hear the seatbelt click if you try to get out. Know that." He threatened. I scanned the backseat under the yard light's beam and noted cigarettes and containers of partially consumed booze while Jack slipped in behind the wheel. I jumped when he screamed, "You got the keys woman?" ...his words run together, almost unintelligible.

"I'm, I'm in the backseat," I stuttered. Did *she* take them—the figure drifting away into the bushes?

Jack hurled himself out of the car, stomped to the house using obscenities I had never heard before, and shrieked savagely, "Dad, Dad…. My keys! You got my keys?!" I unclicked the seatbelt and slipped into the darkness as he pounded on the dead-bolted house door.

"Keys! Unlock the stupid door!! Where are they?"

The big guy, cigar still inserted in his mouth, opened the door, dressed in long johns.

As I raced for the brambles and bushes surrounding the farmstead, I heard another bellow, "No son of mine is going to speak to me that way, boy….."

An argument between father and son escalated and echoed against the trunks of trees soon to be followed by the rumble of a diesel engine. The pickup truck? Feeling as if my chest could explode, I dropped to the ground, exhausted. As I considered who was leaving in the rusted-out pickup, bony fingers gripped my shoulders. I looked up. The woman with wispy hair in a halo circling her aging face pulled me to my feet.

"You?" I panted. "Was it you? Did you take the keys?" My teeth chattered uncontrollably.

She took my quivering hand. I pulled back. She took it again, placed the keys to the Firebird in my palm, and closed my fingers around them as the ancient truck roared from the farmstead.

"He'll be gone lookin' for you. Wait." Her voice was hoarse and urgent. "When I turn off the yard light, take the car."

"And, you?"

"Go!" she said impatiently.

Returning to the car, scanning the house and surrounding trees as I did, I saw her drift in and out of the trees, her hair and light cotton housedress matted against her. It occurred to me that she had done this before. Rescued someone.

I slid into the Pontiac. The farm yard went dark, I started the car, and although I yearned to stomp on the gas, I drove slowly not wanting to make a sound. Without headlights, I left this nightmare. The gas tank registered less than a quarter. My parents' home was too far away. The college dorm? What would that accomplish? I would return to Rusty's and find my friends.

My nerves settled a bit on the way into town. I prayed a lot—going from *help me, help me, God* to *thank you, thank you God*. I felt physically ill. Was it fright, hunger, alcohol, or the combination? Whatever the reason, I could not make any of them go away. I was hungry, I was inebriated, I was scared, I was cold. I pumped up the heat until it blasted at my chest and face and felt somewhat better when I saw city lights in the distance.

I was anxious to get out of his filthy car. I wanted to find my friends. I wanted to take a shower. I wanted to be home. I thought the worst was behind me; however, when I pulled into Rusty's parking lot, I realized it was not. The parking lot was full—a popular college hangout. I circled to the back of the building to discover the rusted out truck. I found another parking spot, removed the keys, and headed to the truck. The driver's side opened with a screech. I slipped my hand across the steering wheel, felt for the keys, and removed them, clenching them in a fist.

I stepped inside Rusty's backdoor and waited as my eyes adjusted to the gloom. Jack was at the bar with my roommate, and I wondered if she was questioning him about my whereabouts. It didn't take me long, however, to realize that this was not the topic of their conversation. He was flirting with her and she was listening. Should I approach them? Should I call the cops? I imagined such a conversation.

*"I'd like to report something."*

*"Yes, your name, please…"*

*"Does it matter? Someone tried to rape me. I jumped from the car and walked to this farm place. It was his parents. I ran. No, I mean, I drove his car into town, and now he's with my roommate."*

*"Mam, I need your name and location. We'll send a security officer out."*

The security officer? The one who asked me if I was okay? Was he still here? What could he do?

My story sounded weak and senseless. But, none of this made Jack innocent. His dad would lie for him. His mother? What might her punishment be when father and son found out she had helped me?

There was a public phone behind the bar. I would be noticed if I used it. With two sets of keys in hand, I waited. Smoke and the smell of alcohol filled the room as my mother's prayer, *God be in my head and in my understanding; God be in my eyes and in my looking…*played repeatedly inside my head while the Bee Gees sang, "Life goin' nowhere, somebody help me. Somebody help me, yeah. Life goin' nowhere, somebody help me, yeah. I'm stayin' alive…"

Still in my coat and wet clothes, the heat and smells from a crowded bar seeped in. Tired, hungry, still fearful, and not having a clue as to what I was supposed to do, like Alice in Wonderland falling down the rabbit hole, I heard the clunk of keys dropping and collapsed on the bar room floor.

"Mandy? Mandy!"

Someone unbuttoned my heavy sweater jacket and fanned me.

"Drunk? Your friend's soused, right?" another said. *Jack*?

"No, she hasn't even been here, in the bar," another mumbled more to herself than anyone else.

I opened my eyes. Curiosity seekers hovered—their faces like some mosaic piece, light filtering through here and there.

"What happened?" another asked.

"Can you get up?" Voices were coming from everywhere.

"Can you get her a glass of water?"

"Where have you been? Where have you been… Where have you been…."

• ✦✦✦✦ •

I graduated college two years later. I never saw Jack again. I stopped hanging out at the bars. I threw myself into homework, student teaching, and building a resume so I could get a good job.

By the time my roommate and I got back to the dorm that night, neither of us was speaking. She was drunk and *embarrassed by my behavior*, as she put it. The experience seemed surreal—like it really hadn't happened or that it had happened but wasn't necessarily as big a deal as I thought it was. I headed to the shower and stayed until the room was filled with steam. Back in the room, my roommate was in deep sleep. I tried bringing it up on the way to the library the following day.

"You know that guy, Jack, you were talking to?" I started.

"What guy?"

"Last night. Jack. At the bar."

"Oh, him, needed a shower, didn't he? Right before you fainted, right? What about him?"

"He offered me a ride home, and I took him up on it."

"What do you mean?" She hesitated, thinking. "When?"

"Remember when you asked me where I was? I was with him, and we ended up on this gravel road and I jumped from the car," I said.

"Why would you do that?" she questioned. "Just a minute, he was at the bar. I was talking to him."

"He attacked me…." I said slowly but emphatically.

"Jack? Why would you think that?" She gave me an accusing glance and picked up her pace to match that of her lab partner ahead of us. "Hey, wait up," she yelled to her.

I grew silent, felt silly, and disgusted—with myself. It was the beginning of me withdrawing from everyone else.

———————•✦✦✦✦•———————

## 1973

I had tried not to remember any of this for years. It was another me I didn't care to relate to. I decided not to date anyone. I developed a dislike for my roommate and spent a lot of time in the library by myself, buried in my studies.

When I finally left the church, it was dark. I was worn out, empty. The raindrops started—cold and pelting. The heavens crackled and then banged, like the sound of a gun blast; the sky rolled back, from one end to the other in a light show. Shivering and shaking almost uncontrollably, I turned on the heat and locked my doors. I hadn't forgotten the incident; I had buried it. And now Sidney's reflections had unearthed my own past.

Back in my mini apartment, I nursed a hot chocolate. I tried music; I tried television. It all seemed so pointless. I finally tackled a stack of vocabulary tests which needed to be handed back on Monday.

The following week was full of lesson plan preparations, teacher meetings related to reading disabilities, and the on-going conferences with individuals in my writing class on the topic *Once Upon a Time*. However, throughout all this sometimes mind-boggling busy-ness, the phrases used by one 16 year-old girl, Sidney, troubled me —*living in a bubble; elephants in the living room;* words like *abuse, mental health issues;* and *the idea that everyone we meet in life, every experience we have, shape us into the person we become*—*those who leave loving imprints, those who leave harmful imprints, leaving forever marks.* The fact that this young woman, Sidney, felt a responsibility to do something about it, that's courage, I thought.

I slept in Saturday morning. Exhaustion is a ready companion of teachers. Trying to ignore the lesson plan book on my kitchen table, I brewed a pot of coffee and scrambled two eggs. Returning to the bedroom, I opened my closet and chose an outfit to wear to church the following day. Looking forward to Sunday, I was able to prepare a literature lesson, take a short bike ride, and trim Mrs. Bisbee's straggling bushes that surrounded her house. I hoped to surprise her when she returned from an out of town visit.

On Sunday, I returned to the church in Downsey dressed in black pants, a black cardigan sweater and white blouse, and hoped to blend in. I was surprised when I drove up to the graveled parking lot at the number of cars. Couples and families trickled up the steps and into the massive structure. Organ music escaped each time the door opened. I slipped into the back pew, picked up the hymnal and turned to the first song designated in the bulletin, "What a Friend We Have in Jesus.".... Eager to get a glimpse of Pastor Warren, this minister with a sermon entitled, "Once Upon a Time", I stretched and scanned the front of the church and then the congregation and realized someone was watching *me*. Embarrassed, I shrunk to a smaller size and listened as a parishioner stepped up the podium and read verses from Genesis and Revelations.

A new voice called the children forward for the children's sermon. Various sizes, shapes, and clothing choices scattered out of the pews, into the center and side aisles, and hurried to the front of the church—some dragging smaller versions of themselves, some trying to catch up with them. Small voices murmured, *Good morning, Pastor Warren, Hi Pastor Warren.*

"Good morning, children, so good to see you," Pastor Warren said, his voice mellow and comforting. "Find a spot. There you go." Children plopped themselves on the floor and then scooted closer and closer to this man until they were at his feet, crowded, elbows and knees touching.

"How many of you like stories?" Pastor Warren asked. All hands raised, even some of the adults in the congregation. "And how do most of the really good stories start?" One or two hands shot up. "Sharon, what do you think? What would be the words?"

"Once upon a time," Sharon answered and shyly giggled.

"You're so right," he replied. "Now, listen carefully, the questions get harder. Are you ready for this one?" A few heads nodded; some were not sure. "With what words do the really good stories end?" Sharon's hand was up immediately. "Let's hear from someone else, Sharon. Anybody? John, your hand is half way up; I bet you have a good answer."

"I think I know," John responded. Pastor Warren's eyes widened expectantly, and he placed the microphone at John's lips. "Is it, *They lived happily ever after?*"

I grew restless, wanting the adult version of the sermon title, and thumbed through the hymnal. Soon, the children returned to their parents with their freckled faces, a runny nose or two, some skipping, some loitering, some not remembering which row their parents were seated in. Being used to high school aged students, I found their expressions and antics comical. After one of them stepped on my foot to get back to his father, I looked up to see the same gentleman who was staring at me earlier. I slouched back in my seat as Pastor Warren ambled up to the pulpit, situated the microphone, and perused his congregation.

"The children were right," he began. "We all love stories, and *Once upon a time* has been a story starter for generations. Why even Genesis 1:1 which begins with the words, *In the beginning…* could read *Once upon a time* God created the heavens and earth." The minister paused for effect. "God said, let there be light, and there was light. He said, let the land produce vegetation, seed-bearing plants, and trees on the land. And, it was so. God asked for lights in the expanse of the sky and that the water teem with living creatures and that birds fly across the expanse of the sky. There were living creatures on the land, and then God said, let us make man in our image to rule over the fish of the sea and the birds of the air, over the livestock, over all the earth. God saw all this and thought that it was good." He paused. "Once upon a time…"

Pastor Warren pulled out his hanky, wiped his nose briefly, but kept his eyes on his notes. The congregation grew restless; someone dropped a hymnal. My mother's words and phrases swirled inside my head. *Once upon a time we had a baby girl, once upon a time Mandy had a grand birthday party, once upon a time my baby girl went off to college, once upon a time my little girl became a teacher* and without me allowing my brain to stop, the words came *once upon a time my baby girl was sexually assaulted*. Words, I did not want to use.

Studying, preparing for a job, teaching, distractions small and large consumed my life until my perceptions of what had happened were skewed, clogged, buried. I stood, ready to leave as Pastor Warren cleared his throat and looked at the back of the congregation.

"God made everything good. Human sin spoiled it. He alone is sovereign and He alone will direct history for the good of His people. Whether it's your own personal seemingly impossible dilemma that you feel you can do nothing about or whether it's your concern over what is happening in our world, remember that God can sustain you in all things. He will direct history for the good of His people." Mesmerized, I sat down.

"There is incredible unity in the Bible. Most of us don't see it. After all, there are sixty-six books and it's easy to get distracted in the many stories, but there is a running theme of redemption from Genesis to God's redemption of mankind made known in Revelation."

I was aware of the fact that most people found the book of Revelation scary, untouchable, with its apocalyptic pronouncements. And, here, Pastor Warren paints a happy ending?

"The last chapter of Revelation tells us that Jesus is coming. Verse 13 reads, *I am the Alpha and the Omega, the First and the Last, the Beginning and the End*. Talk about, And they lived happily ever after? What more could we ask than living with God, Our Creator, in eternity?"

"As Jeremiah 29:11 tells us, *For I know the plans I have for you… plans to prosper you and not to harm you, plans to give you hope and a future. Then you will call upon me and come and pray to me, and I will listen to you.*"

I took the pencil available in the pew rack and wrote Jeremiah 29:11. *For I know the plans I have for you…*

"No matter your dilemma, no matter your own personal *once upon a time*, there will be a *and they lived happily ever after*." Again, Pastor Warren paused, this time perusing the congregation, nodding a yes. "With prayers and praise and thanksgiving, let us believe and trust. Amen."

As the congregation answered their own *Amen*, I could no longer sit still. I passed the ushers with the collection plates and clutched the rail as I walked down the cement steps to my car. My hand shook as I unlocked my car and dropped into the driver's seat. It continued to shake as I turned the key in the ignition. I heard the congregation sing *Amazing grace, how sweet the sound that saved a wretch like me…* as I pulled from the parking lot.

Thoughts from my own personal *Once upon a time*, thoughts from Sidney's assignment, and phrases from Pastor Warren's sermon churned inside my head until I felt emotionally and physically drained. I thought about going back to bed when I arrived at my apartment. Mrs. Bisbee was still gone, and I felt very alone, isolated. It's not like we hung out together or spent that much time together. It's just that she was a presence in this big house and sometimes that was all I needed.

I busied myself with cutting up vegetables for a pot of soup. While it simmered on the small, gas stove, I dusted everything in every room from top to bottom—lampshades, mop boards, the few knickknacks I had acquired. When I got to the dining room table, I picked up the bulletin from church, thought about tossing it, and then checked out next Sunday's sermon title: *Before He Made the World*. And knew I would be back in church. I finished the afternoon by recording grades and vacuuming. Hearing Mrs. Bisbee's car on the driveway, I hurried downstairs and met her at the door.

"I have a pot of soup on," I said. "Want to share supper with me?" She followed me up the steps. We talked about the weather, her plans for new shutters for the house. I told her I had gone to church and heard Pastor Warren speak leaving out my emotional roller-coaster on the way home and my own private thoughts.

"Oh, he's very popular around here," she said. "I'm sorry I missed it. He tells it like it is, but ever so lovingly." Remembering the bulletin I had stashed beside my purse in the hallway, I got up to get it, thinking she may be interested in the announcements and order of service. She perused it.

"His sermon titles always get my curiosity going," she said. "*Once Upon a Time*. We all have our stories, don't we?" She closed her eyes for several moments before returning to the next week's events. "I see I have a circle meeting on Thursday evening. We're studying Paul's words to Timothy. The guidelines Paul offers seem at times ancient. But I think it narrows down to heavenly responsibilities no matter what our role in life is."

"Heavenly responsibilities?" I questioned. It was a nice-sounding phrase, but I wondered what Mrs. Bisbee meant.

"Simply being aware of what others are going through; being

compassionate, respectful, and considerate is a start," she answered. "If we're all wrapped up in ourselves, it's pretty difficult to be aware of anyone else's circumstances."

I pulled some peanut butter cookies from a store-bought package and asked if she would like some hot tea.

"Sounds perfect. I usually have tea after my evening meal." As I pulled two tea bags from a tin, she continued to read the bulletin. "Like I said, those sermon titles. Next Sunday's title is *Even Before He Made the World*. Don't you wonder about that one?"

Before slipping under the covers, I got on my knees and asked God for forgiveness for not dealing with the darkness from my past. I also thanked him for all the goodness I had in my life, my parents, the co-workers, the students at school, and Mrs. Bisbee who had given me a very pleasant ending to my day. The words from "Amazing Grace" filled my heart and I soon drifted off to cozy sleep.

------------ +◆◆◆◆+ ------------

After school one day, a patrol car sat next to mine in the parking lot. I assumed he was waiting for someone else, but the officer was soon within a foot of my backside as I unloaded the unchecked homework in the backseat of my car.

"Miss Herman? Mandy Herman?" he asked.

I stood up and closed the car door before turning to face him. He was tall and nice looking. Even though he was in uniform, I recognized him as the man in church who had his eyes on me off and on.

"Yes, I'm Mandy Herman. Can I help you? Is something wrong?" I immediately thought of Mrs. Bisbee. Had she fallen? Had a stroke? Had I somehow unthinkingly broken a law?

"No, nothing wrong, Mandy, ah Miss Herman," he replied, and I realized he was embarrassed, blushing. "This may seem forward, but I'm new in town, saw you in church last Sunday, and wondered if you'd like to have coffee sometime."

I kept staring at him; I didn't know what to say. I should've been embarrassed myself, but it turned out I was confused, so I ended up saying something most would consider inappropriate.

"Are you sure?" I asked and finally did blush. He laughed. Then, I laughed.

"Well, I've been thinking about asking you for weeks," he said, his right hand rubbing the back of his neck. We both looked up as a group of starlings escaped from a nearby tree, wheeling and darting above us. When I brought my attention back to earth, I caught him staring at me. "Yes, I'm sure," he answered.

"Okay. Yes, I'd like to have coffee sometime," I answered.

"Saturday? Let's meet at Coffee & More. 9 o'clock."

I nodded and smiled and watched him walk back to the patrol car and then yelled, "Stop!" He jerked his head up in surprise.

"Sorry," I said. "I don't know your name."

———————— ·••••·• ————————

I dressed casually, slacks and a pullover sweater. Brushing my hair back in a ponytail, I noted a few straggling gray hairs. My mother was totally gray in her early thirties, so it seemed I was headed in that direction. With an application of mascara and a little lip ice, I grabbed a light-weight jacket, and walked the few blocks to Coffee & More. As I neared the little café, I noticed through the window that Mike was standing just inside the door. Like a bouncer, I thought, and appreciated his enthusiasm.

"Good morning," he said opening the door for me. Khaki pants, a plaid pressed shirt, and a hint of English Leather greeted me. We found a booth by a window. A young waitress approached us.

"Hey, Officer Stevens, you're lookin' good today," she said looking from Mike to me and back again at Mike. We both ordered coffee, black, and huge caramel rolls. They arrived warm and gooey.

"Sorry, I didn't introduce myself the other day; kinda' rude, right?" Mike started the conversation. His look was speculating, like *I can't believe you don't remember me.*

"I saw you at church, but we never talked. I left a little early," I explained remembering the sermon "Once Upon a Time".

"I'm never disappointed in Pastor Warren's message," Mike said and took a bite. His lips started a smile that grew wide as if he were spontaneously inspired. "Okay, listen up, Mandy. Once upon a time, in another world and another place, we knew each other."

"What? Come on…." I replied and shook my head. "Another world? Another place?" I was starting to like this guy. We could kid each other. I felt safe and comfortable with him.

"You really don't remember me, do you? I'm hurt," he said, again, teasing.

"Okay, I saw you in church or you saw me," I replied. "If there's another world and another place, you'll have to fill me in."

"Does Journalism 101 ring a bell?" he asked tentatively. "University of Iowa, Adler Building, top floor, corner room. You sat by the window. I sat in the back corner and admired you from afar." Mike studied me and waited for a reaction.

"You're serious," I replied. "That must have been my sophomore year." And, then, I grew bold. "You waited this long to ask me out?" The café grew quiet. I realized that the question and my rising voice had gotten the attention of others around us, including the waitress. I murmured a *sorry* to Mike.

"Not a problem," he answered with a smirk and took his last bite of gooey roll. "Want more coffee?"

I watched him carry our two cups to the coffee bar and refill them. He possessed a quiet confidence, walked assertively. Others watched him. I imagined us spending more time together: a movie, a dinner date. My parents would like him. Intrigued and interested, I told myself to *stop*. *You just met this guy, Mandy.* I took a deep breath and told my imagination to take a hike.

"Black, right?" Mike asked, setting the refilled cup before me.

"Right. Thank you," I replied. "What's with the journalism class? You became a cop."

"I've always had an interest in writing. In fact, English was my favorite class in high school. Needed another English credit and the Journalism 101 class looked like something I could handle."

"I'm sorry I didn't notice you," I apologized and wished I had.

"There was another time," he said as he settled himself back in the booth we shared, this time stirring in a teaspoon of sugar. "Rusty's."

"Rusty's? You mean the bar in Iowa City?" I sat up straight and crossed my arms in front of me. "Wow, you got a great memory, Journalism 101 and now Rusty's? Did you go there often?"

"Several times during the week and every other weekend," Mike said and looked out the window. A couple of kids raced by on their bikes. Mike didn't look like the kind of guy who partied through college. So, I looked away, too. Others were ordering coffees to go. The little café started to empty.

"I'm sorry I brought it up," Mike said.

"No need to," I replied and wondered what he might be hiding.

"I worked at Rusty's as a bouncer while I was in college. Wasn't the best job, but the pay was good, and it didn't interfere with my class schedule."

I knew there was more that he wanted to say. I just didn't know if I wanted to hear it.

"So, that's what inspired you to become a police officer?" I asked.

"Maybe. I already had ideas. My uncle's a cop. Always admired him." I nodded and hoped he would keep talking—more about the route he had taken to become a certified police officer. However, he ventured in a direction I wasn't prepared for.

"I noticed you the night you left with that guy, Jack." He waited for my reaction. I stared at his folded hands on the table and then mine. "I already had an interest in you because of you being in the Journalism class," he explained. "I wanted to help but didn't want to interfere. When you returned, I could tell something was wrong, but you didn't know me... I didn't know how to proceed." Mike covered his mouth with his left hand as if to stop the words from coming. I looked out the window and thought about getting up and walking home. Would he follow? Did I want him to, expect him to?

"You knew *Jack*?" I wondered out loud.

"Everyone knew Jack," he answered. "We knew about him, but no one ever turned him in or pressed charges." Memories of Jack and that night made me feel stupid, naïve, lousy. I didn't like these feelings. I was a competent, respected teacher and was having morning coffee with the town cop. The conversation was going in a direction that frustrated me.

"I don't know what to say," I whispered and shook my head.

"I'm sorry," Mike replied. "Maybe, it was the wrong time to bring it up."

"It's okay," I answered but was disappointed that he had done so. Pastor Warren started me thinking about the whole thing last Sunday, and now this…. "Is that why you asked me to meet for coffee? You want information on Jack?" The fleeting thought of Jack still being out there, picking up innocent girls in his Pontiac Firebird, and sexually assaulting them sickened me.

If it was possible for a big guy like Mike, all six feet and close to 200 pounds, to look startled, he was.

"It's not looking good for me, right now, is it?" Mike said. A red line started at the top of his shirt collar and worked its way up until his entire face was covered. He was angry. He cleared his throat several times before stating emphatically, "In answer to your question, absolutely not. This is not about Jack. I thought… I'm not sure what I thought. Perhaps, it was simply that I thought you may have remembered me." I thought he might get up and walk out. In a few moments, our time together had gone from light-hearted to agonizing.

"Can you walk me home?" I asked. "I know you drove, but I'd like to walk." It was a quiet walk. In spite of our conversation at Coffee & More, it felt good to be at his side, our arms gently brushing each other with each step. I asked him to come up to the apartment and offered him a glass of water. He sat at the dining room table. The talk turned to chit chat, the weather, Mrs. Bisbee's generous reputation in town, the busy-ness of a country church just outside Downsey. A couple of hours slipped by.

Mike and I shared the leftover pot of soup for lunch. I confessed my feelings of total naivety and stupidity over what had happened so long ago with Jack without giving details, and that these feelings were on-going. He reached for my hand, our fingers interlaced, as I told him of my recent trip to Downsey, my short visit with Jack's mother, and how I was concerned about her well-being. He listened without judgement and offered no advice. He simply listened, his eyes never leaving mine.

I eventually dozed off on the couch. When I awoke, I realized Mike had covered me with the afghan that had been draped on another easy chair. There had been no *goodbyes*, no *see you again*. I felt empty.

Sunday morning, I got up early, ate a bowl of hot oatmeal, and pulled on the most comfortable clothes I could pick from the back of the closet. I needed to go home. Mom and Dad greeted me with hugs and kisses. After catching-up on family and community news and sharing a pot roast meal followed with lemon meringue pie, I told them I had something to share with them that was not good. I briefly described the story of that night at Rusty's, my poor decision, and how I had tried to bury the whole incident. My mom lovingly told me that she knew something had happened. I had changed over-night she said, and, then she asked *why didn't you tell us? We could have helped.* Their love was unconditional and on-going. Their hugs, kisses, and compassionate tears were the medicine I needed.

---

Mike was in the parking lot beside his patrol car after school on Monday. I was glad to see him and wondered how I could feel so close to him in such a short time. I had shared things with him that no one else knew, and here he was waiting for me. He helped me put the bundles from school in the backseat before saying, "Sorry, I left without saying goodbye."

"Thanks for covering me up with the afghan."

"I looked for you at church. Sleep in?" he asked.

"I spent the day with my parents," I replied. "It had been awhile. Mom's pot roast was calling, I guess."

"I've got an hour for break time, want to talk?" Mike asked.

"Sure. My apartment. It's a hot chocolate kind of day. Mom sent ginger snaps home with me." He followed me, and I wondered what the small community of Solon would say if they noticed Mike following me, dressed in his uniform, driving a police vehicle.

Mrs. Bisbee greeted us at the front door as she swept a few leaves from the porch. "Hi, Mike, Mandy," she stated brightly. "Great day, isn't it?"

"Want to come up for hot chocolate and cookies?" I asked her.

"Not today," she said and winked. "Got a late start on my list of things to do."

Mike sat at the table and pulled out yesterday's Sunday bulletin. "Well, he did it again," Mike stated.

"What? You mean Pastor Warren?" I placed the hot chocolate on the table along with a plate of ginger snaps.

"You remember the sermon title?" he asked.

"Sure. 'Even Before He Made the World.'"

"Well, I'm not going to give you a summary or anything. But it's based on Ephesians 1:4. I'll let you read it later."

Before Mike left that day, he thanked me for the cookies and hot chocolate and the extras I had placed in a bag for him to enjoy at his house. I followed him to the door and wanted to run my fingertips across his wide shoulders and the dark curls at the nape of his neck. He turned and we were face to face, within inches of each other.

"I'll see you soon?" he said, a twinkle in his eyes.

"Yeah, you'll see me soon," I answered. With one hand he held the cookie plate; with the other he pulled me close to him. I rested my cheek on his chest, felt his warmth, and hugged him with both arms. Yes, I would see him again.

I counted his footsteps with each step he took down to the front door. Through the front window, I watched him walk to the police car and get in. I thought about his one-armed hug as I cleared the table and picked up the bulletin to read Ephesians 1:4. *Even before he made the world, God loved us and chose us in Christ to be holy and without fault in his eyes. God decided in advance to adopt us into his own family by bringing us to himself through Jesus Christ. This is what he wanted to do, and it gave him great pleasure.* I reflected on this. God does not want my self-condemnation. He wants me to be a part of the family of Jesus Christ. In this family, my words, actions, and heart are to be aligned with His. In this family, I have a responsibility to reflect my love to others, to be aware, considerate, compassionate.

1975

Mother whispered into my ear as her tears trickled down my neck, "Once upon a time, my little girl got married." I kissed her cheek.

"Love you, Mandy," Dad said and gave me a bear hug, his own eyes brimming.

There were no bridesmaids, no groomsmen—just me and Mike, our parents, Mrs. Bisbee, and a few friends. We each have had our *once upon a time.* There are no guarantees on *they lived happily ever after.* But, I think Mike and I have a good start. Due to Mike's encouragement, I shared my story about that night with Jack to the county sheriff who will assist in an on-going investigation. The Department of Human Services was contacted regarding Jack's mother's environment and health. Living happily ever after? There are no guarantees unless we're talking about God's plan for a life in an eternity that only He understands. Knowing this will get you through all the other stuff.

Oh, you're probably wondering about Sidney, the young woman and her rendition of "Once Upon a Time." She accepted a scholarship at the University of Iowa with a double major in mind—social work and journalism. She's already made a difference and with her heart and perspective on life, she'll continue by the grace of God to do so.

# PROVIDENCE

With cup of tea in hand, I settle on the porch swing. Tree tops shift with an over-head breeze. Tattered flags hang from nearby porches, their houses silent. No garage doors opening and closing, no cars rumbling by on the street. Typically, on this morning, Independence Day, small trucks head to the fairgrounds tugging parade floats in preparation for the annual spectacle in our small town, Providence. Inhaling cool morning air and the rare tranquility, I am puzzled.

I sense something overhead and spot a snowy flourish above the ancient tree in the front yard. It is a swarm of butterflies and not a breeze that troubles the tree tops. I whack away the single butterfly that has landed on my t-shirt, re-enter the house, fill a bowl with cornflakes, and head for the table by the deck door. Outlaw and Gangsta, the backyard neighbor's dogs, are usually out mucking up their yard; however, no dogs today, but there are the butterflies, again, fingering the tree tips.

I rinse my bowl in the sink and give the house a once-over. Everything is in place, exactly as I left it the night before: Mama's quilt folded in a square on the couch, my pen parallel to my black journal on my desk, and Ethan's framed photo on the coffee table. His picture is there, but mostly I try not to look at it. It's gotten easier over the years. But, when someone you thought loved you, rejects you, the hurt never really goes away. It just prances around your heart as the years drift by and every once in a while, takes a stab.

Intrigued by the stillness, I leave the house and start to walk—something that has become an effort. At Gas & Shop, I stop to rest. There are cars, but they are empty as is the store. Thinking some tragedy happened during the night, I lumber a few more blocks to our small town urgent-care clinic. The welcome desk is bare; the halls are hollow. I amble to the church across the street. Light slips in between pillars and casts eerie shadows across the pews. With goosebumps peppering my skin, I turn homeward—jeopardizing myself with each unsteady step. On the way, I notice the empty parking lot of the grocery store with weeds growing through the cracks.

The man who lives next door to me works for the city; maybe everyone lost their power and… I knock. I turn the door knob and yell into the house, "Anyone home?" Folded laundry in a basket, a medicine bottle on the countertop, dirty dishes in the sink. I turn to another house across the street and step in. Left-over pizza stagnates on the table. No tick-tock of the clock. No air-conditioning humming.

Back home, my mind races. *Where is everyone? What happened? Who did this?* The mailbox is typically empty, but I check anyway. Nothing. The television is unresponsive; my phone is dead; the kitchen faucet offers only drips. By now, the silence overwhelms me and yet it is paradoxically loud—ranging from ringing to roaring inside my head. My pulse thumps.

The sun sets; the day grows dim and then dark. My legs are heavy weights, but my heart takes off on a run. I breathe in and out, in and out, clutch Ethan's picture to my core, wrap myself in Mama's quilt on the couch, and hope that this will all go away.

Exhausted, my chin drops to my chest, it jolts up; this pattern is endless until a shrill whistle disrupts the night. I put two and two together; my heart stumbles. There's no one in my small town; not a thing moving; but, now, a train? Its existence slips in and out of the imperfections and crevices of my house: the wheels boisterous clickety-clacking, the unnerving light. I cover my ears as it passes just two blocks away until, once more, muteness penetrates.

Dawn materializes somehow. Sleep deprived my body rebels with each movement; a dull throbbing fills my head. I lumber outside wanting the butterflies. Watching them linger above the trees makes me feel better. A master of metamorphosis, their peaceful demeanor and graceful movements remind me that in ancient Greek, the word for butterfly was *psyche* which translated meant *soul*. There is a small town in Mexico which believes that butterflies are the returning souls of the deceased. I think of Papa dying of cancer and Mama taken by the same disease that now plagues me. Ethan was another… But, I do not think of Ethan being gone: he is out there, somewhere, yearning to rescue me.

Deeply disturbed with my circumstances, I do something out of character: I break into houses. They are all devoid of life. Even the clocks; each has stopped at 11:59 p.m.

Because the train tracks were the only sign of recent life, I am drawn to them. No longer self-conscious about my awkward limp, a result of my ailment that has become a challenge over time, I head for them. Dropping beside the railway line, I examine the tracks, feel the sleek rails, and start to question everything in my life. Could I have been wrong about others? Could I have been mistaken even about myself? How had I gotten so caught up in me? I didn't even know my neighbors' names. I was too bitter to forgive Ethan before he left with another. I resented losing my parents early in life. I was angry about my illness. I viewed myself as damaged goods.

The silence is mind-boggling, heavy, insulting. My breathing, my heart beat, my brain storming are a tempest. Desolate, the tears tumble, and a single butterfly lands on my wet face. Instinctively, I brush it away.

Back home, I pack Mama's quilt, clutch Ethan's picture to my heart, and struggle back to the tracks; mind unglued, body drained. As daylight drifts to murky dusk, I wait. On my knees, I search the stars and planets until I feel the ground beneath me vibrate and sense a faint sliver of light peering through a settling fog.

The train's eye draws close, probing its surroundings like a monster cyclops. Trembling, I scan the train as it passes. Instead of tank cars and grain hoppers, these are passenger cars filled with lifeless forms. A high-pitched, ear-piercing blast rattles me completely, and the engine thunders past.

The train journeys on through desolate fields and around the bend until only the faintest of murmurs can be detected, like a whisper lost in far-off clouds. Surrounded by darkness and soft breezes, I return to my house with questions that cannot be put into words. Still clutching the quilt and photograph, I drop on the couch and curl up into a ball as gentle thunder rolls and a lightning strike illuminates the room.

I am roused by a tapping on the front door.

Rooted to the couch, I cannot speak, but someone does.

"Adriel?"

My mouth is dry, cracked.

"Adriel, I've come for you," a gentle voice says.

"Why?" I ask. ... and something ripples inside me.

With an angel voice, she explains, "You've been summoned by name." But, I do not believe in angels. "Please, come; there's not much time," she encourages.

"There is no time," I whisper. "Everything has stopped."

"You're right, Adriel; time has stopped."

"Please go away," I plead. "I don't understand any of this. There's nothing left."

"This is when miracles happen," she reassures me. "Please, come."

"I don't believe in miracles." And then I add, "I'm afraid," knowing I have rarely in my life felt courage.

As if she knew my thoughts, she replies, "You have often been afraid of being abandoned, afraid of being incompetent, afraid of being you." She pauses. "Courage is when you realize that something greater is at stake."

With Ethan's picture against my breast and wrapped in Mama's quilt, I take baby steps towards the door. "How do you know all this?" I ask.... "I'm so tired."

"Walking in death's shadow is wearing," she replies with a sigh.

Feeling I am one misstep from being suspended on the edge of nowhere, I crack open the door. Are those wings attached to her back? Her hair is floating. She is there and yet isn't.

"How did you know my name?" I wonder out loud.

"We've known your name since the beginning of time."

Confused, I ask, "What do you want me to do?" And with this question, something reassuring washes through me. I open the door wide. A single white butterfly flutters in and rests on my shoulder, right above my heart.

"Kyrie Eleison," the angel-like figure replies and if a vapor-like thing can act relieved, she does.

"Kyrie....?"

"No worries." She beams. "Just follow me. You won't need anything." Although I do not intentionally drop them, Mama's quilt and Ethan's picture are gone; my black journal sits abandoned on the coffee table.

With each step, my aches and pains slip away. I know where we are going: the tracks. She strides beside me. A hum—a musical pulsation of sorts—comes from her and the universe at the same time. A gentle harmony of a thousand instruments courses through my vessels giving voice to a beauty inside me as white butterflies gather around us.

"It's not time for the train, yet," I tell her and feel like I could fly.

"Don't forget, we're on the Kingdom's Calendar," she responds.

I sense the train; I feel its synchronization with the thousand instruments and the dancing butterflies. The entire thing is surrounded by light with **Providence** printed on its side. It slows and stops beside us.

"Providence?" I ask.

"Of course," my angel answers. "Welcome." She bows slightly and gestures with her arms.

I take the steps, open the door, and feel transformed. Is this life once again? Or is it simply always-as-it-was-intended-to-be....

I turn to her and want to know, "Your name?"

"Mercy," she answers and vanishes.

Passengers on the train quietly greet me with smiles and gentle caresses. Someone offers me a seat by a window. Feeling protected, accepted, and new, I watch the passing fields of green, the flowers blossoming brilliance. The train click-clacks on the track—the sound of soft-snapping-fingers—and my world begins reorganizing itself.

There are no yesterdays, no tomorrows.

I know I am free.

Providence?

Now the LORD

Is the Spirit,

And where the Spirit of the LORD is,

There is freedom.

And we, who with unveiled faces,

All reflect the LORD'S glory,

Are being transformed into His likeness

With ever increasing glory,

Which comes from the LORD who is the Spirit.

2 Corinthians 3:17-18

# Divine Plan

When the Creator established sky and sea

He knew about me.

With my name written on His hand, a little mystery,

He knew who I could be.

Formed in His image, created to be free,

I grew wild, weary, unable to see—

O'Lord, my God, I have no worth without thee.

But by your grace while on bended knee

Someday, I'll understand what
You meant for me to be...

...and humbly start eternity.

# DISCUSSION QUESTIONS

*Summoned*

1. There are some issues we cannot resolve. There are some issues that offer no closure. You've heard of the expression, "Let go and let God." How can this apply to each main character in the novelette?

Emilie Fischer

Joseph Turner

2. We all make senseless decisions at one time or another. Think of an unwise decision you made that could have been life-threatening. Looking back, were there times when you understand now that you were protected by God? What significance does the cardinal play in the narrative? Discuss the Hebrew meaning of Michael?

3. Is there anything unresolved in your life? Can you surrender it to God?

## Jacqueline's Story

1. "Jacqueline's Story" is a spin-off of the novel, *Do Not Be Deceived*. Jacqueline, the mother, leaves early in the narrative and doesn't return until the end of the book. This short story is what happened to Jacqueline. Under what circumstances would a mother leave a child in a potentially unfit or even dangerous situation?

2. Consider those parents who live in your community who some might deem as unfit. How might you view them differently after reading "Jacqueline's Story?" What should be our Christian response?

## Ramona's Visitor

1. Is there an elderly person who has been an inspiration to you? In what way? Take your time to visit a shut-in or aging relative soon. Give a gift of your time; it will give you a gift, also.

2. Do you think James Freeman will return to Titus Assisted Living? If so, for what reason?

3. What do you admire about Ramona?

## *Hope*

1. This is the only story in the book that has no scripture until the conclusion. What other Biblical references might be appropriate? Discuss 1 Peter 5:8. Discuss Jeremiah 29:1.

2. In our world, brokenness seems to be a given: broken hearts, broken relationships, dreams lost. How does each character in "Hope" indicate brokenness?

Bonnie

Hank

Hope

3. Discuss possible tragic endings to the story. Discuss possible positive endings to the story.

## Norma's Class Reunion

1. If Norma had a problem, what would it be? How did this impact the way she lived her life?

2. Is it possible that someone like Tim could change her life's direction?

3. Speculate on their future together....

## Once Upon a Time

1. The *Me, Too* movement, a movement against sexual harassment and sexual assault, is a prevalent topic. What do we need to keep in mind when we hear these stories or recall our own?

2. Discuss *The Fruits of the Spirit* and how the world would be different if everyone lived with these qualities.

3. What is the scariest thing that ever happened to you? How did you learn from it?

## *Providence*

1. Adriel knew the names of the dogs in her backyard but no one else in her neighborhood. What does this reveal about her character, her personality?


2. Each name has a meaning significantly tied to the story's theme. Research Hebrew name definitions and discuss how they fit in the sequence of events.


Adriel


Ethan


Mercy


Providence


3. Why is Providence both the name of the town and on the side of the train?

4. The Lord's Prayer states "…Thy kingdom come, Thy will be done on earth as it is in heaven." Can you relate this to the story? If so, how?

5. Where do you think everyone has gone?

## Divine Plan

1. Isn't it awesome that God knew about you and me before Creation? Perhaps you want to look at yourself in another way knowing this….

2. Discuss the word eternity and what it means to you.

3. What emotion does the poem project? Humility? Why may that be important?

4. How does the poem indicate God's power?

Printed in the United States
By Bookmasters